The Last Time I Saw Love (Revised)

A Christian Romance   Novel

Lucy Heath

A Novel Thing, LLC

Other Romance Novels
by
Lucy Heath

Rachel's Forbidden Love

The Reunion

Pastor Q and Donna
(A Christmas Surprise)

Matters *of the* Heart Seasons of Love
Winter: (The Uncertain Heart)

The Best Christmas Ever

A Novel Thing, LLC, Revised edition © 2021
Cover design: Q2 Entertainment & Management ®

Note to the Reader

While this novel is set against the backdrop of a real city name, and may mention characters that appear to be realistic to the reader, the characters and their dwelling places are all fictional. They do not in any way depict any known persons, or their lifestyles. The intent of their faith is not to be in competition with any other religious group, but only to portray what the author believes to be Christian principles for her characters to draw from, and to live by.

Acknowledgements

I am most grateful to the Lord, the members of my immediate family, my pastor, my church, and many other friends who encouraged me in the vision I have to pen these novels. I thank God for those around me who think it not robbery to faithfully live the Christian Faith.

Thanks

My thanks to those who have shared recipes that have been handed down in their family from grandmothers to mothers; and now are passed down to them. We wanted to include these recipes of *love* for those readers who are just starting out, or may not have had parents, and grandparents who passed on time-tested favorites to them.

Niveta Hoskins, Francine Baise
Laniese Heath, Mary Chantrè
Deborah Asbury, and 'Miss' Lucy

Chapter 1

Connie parked her car in the driveway, and sat for a few minutes before turning the key off. It was mid-July and the air-conditioning in the car felt good, but she was on a tight budget, and she knew that just sitting there letting the car run like that would use up her gas. Reluctantly, Connie turned off the key, and rolled down the two front windows. Her brother promised to stop by the old house and help her sort through a few things. But, knowing him; his two o'clock promise would be closer to three, and if he said he'd meet you about three o'clock, it would most likely end up being closer to five in the afternoon. Why were some people like that?

Connie hated to criticize her own brother so much, but his nonchalant ways irked her. For just once she would like for him to be a man of his word. She looked down at the watch on her wrist. He was already twenty-five minutes late. Well, what could she expect! He was the baby of the family; and always got away with *murder*.

After a few more pouts, she opened the driver's side door and got out of the car. She thought wearing the tank top and a pair of *Bermuda* shorts would make her feel cooler, but they weren't really helping much. Connie stewed for a few seconds more looking up and down the road hoping against hope that Edmund would be rolling

11

down the partially paved street; no such luck. She moved towards the steps not wanting to linger outside too long. It may have been selfish of her but, she just didn't feel like socializing with any of her mother's old neighbors; especially the
'*nosy*' ones.

Connie climbed the steps and scanned the width of the extra-long veranda. The porch swing was to the far left, and the rest of the screened-in porch held a host of wicker furniture sets, and comfortable chairs. Feeling a lump forming in the back of her throat, she quickly removed the house key from her purse and inserted it in the front door lock. Safely inside she rested her back against the closed door. Connie shut her eyes, and took in a few deep breaths. *'You can do this'*, she said to herself. *'You can do this.'*

Mother Minnie Webster passed away right after the family reunion last May. Mournfully, Connie remembered
it was less than three weeks after the family all got together (July 7, 1970). The family sensed something wasn't quite right with her. They couldn't put their finger on it, but whatever it was, their mother wasn't willing to say. Of course, they all questioned her about her health. They noticed that she looked a little tired, but she told them she had gone to the doctor, and now she was taking some vitamins, and watching her diet. All that may have been true; but they found out later... much too late, it was only half of the story.

Mrs. Webster was diagnosed with a rare form of congenital heart failure, and at best; they later found out from Dr. Brown, she was told she had only three to six months before her heart would give out altogether. Sometimes, Connie thought, *'At best... our best just isn't good enough'.* She tried not to mix bitterness with feelings of guilt that sifted through her resurfacing grief. Connie headed for the armchair in the living room, and let the tears flow as she lowered herself onto the cushion.

It took the family about a year working with the attorneys regarding their mother's Will. The family had to decide what to do about the house and the property. Until that was decided, they paid the taxes, and shut off the utilities.

Connie knew she had been sitting in the chair for a while, but she wasn't sure how long. A quick peek at her watch let her know it was close to three o'clock. It also let her know that her baby brother probably was not going to show. She thought maybe she could give him a call to see if he had left his apartment. Connie dabbed at her still wet cheeks with the end of her tank top, and stood to her feet. There were two phones in the house. One was mounted on the kitchen wall next to the light-switch, and the other one was in her parent's bedroom. *Wow, in her parent's bedroom.*

In her present befuddlement Connie could not remember if the telephone service was on, or still off. She remembered having had the electricity and water turned back on, but she could not remember about the telephone service. Taking the few steps through the dining room to the kitchen answered her question. No dial tone!

Connie pulled the little '*To Do*' list out of her pocket.
A quick sweep of the list answered another question.
It was one of the things Edmund was supposed to do.
'*Another responsibility that falls on my shoulders*' she
thought out loud. *Why is it that every task the younger
ones don't want to do falls on my shoulders? Ever since I
could remember; all I ever heard was, "Remember you're
the oldest".* She did not mean for her thoughts to mock her
mother's voice, but they did, and now she felt ashamed.

Since she was in the kitchen, Connie flipped on the
switch, and the kitchen lit up. Before she could move,
some of her childhood memories engulfed her mind. She
heard voices around the table at supper time; the clanging
of pots and pans while her mother cooked, and the
'tee-hee' of giggling girls when she and her sister washed
the dishes. She could still see Olivia, (Leve*e*) for short,
standing on an upside down wooden crate with Mom's
apron tied around her chest. Mom and Pop Webster
started their children out young in assuming household
duties, and responsibilities.

Connie started at the kitchen sink when she was
only four years old. Then, she was the one who stood on
the crate next to her mother. She was only allowed to
handle the silverware and saucers (no sharp knives, or
glassware).

At that time her mother let her pretend she was
washing

the dishes, but mainly she was slopping the dish rag up and down in the warm sudsy water, and making a big mess.

The reflections of that vision brought a smile to Connie's face, and yet–another pang to her heart.

How could someone have a medical problem that existed from birth, and not know it? Did Pop know? Didn't she go to the doctors for checkups and a physical? *Sure. I knew she did,* Connie thought. *As a matter of fact, she went at least twice a year, even when she was in her thirties and forty's. So, how could she have not known?* Connie was becoming angry again. So, she had to stop dwelling on the subject. For most of her childhood years all she heard from both of her parents was; *"You are the oldest. You should know better." Well, didn't that same thing go for parents who were older, and should know better than their kids?"*

"Okay, she said aloud. "I have to get a hold of my feelings and emotions. First I was angry, and now I'm playing the blame game. I'm familiar enough with the different stages of grief, and know that these emotions were some of its patterns." Yet, Connie thought, *both of my parents are gone. First it was dad, who never fully recovered from the car accident four years ago when he was blindsided by a drunk driver. We prayed, and prayed, and then prayed some more.* Her Mama almost lived at the hospital while he was in a coma. When they got to the sixth week mark, their hope was fading and their faith began to weaken. But then by some miracle of heaven, while their mother sat there talking with him (as

15

she usually did), he opened his eyes. Edmund and Olivia rushed to the hospital right after their mom's phone call. Connie lived out of town, and had the farthest to travel.

By the time she arrived, her dad was gone. Her mother said it seemed like he woke up just long enough to say that he was going home. He told her how much he loved the Lord, and he loved her, and all of his children. Mom said after that; his eyes fluttered shut, and his hand fell softly from its grip in hers.

The family was still in the room when I came through the door, but he was gone. *My dad really was gone*! Connie was heartbroken, and cried with her brother and sister; but her heart ached even more because she felt that she had been cheated out of her last chance to say goodbye.

"Fifteen minutes! She said. I couldn't believe it. How cruel time could be… just fifteen minutes earlier, And I would have had my chance to tell my Dad how much I loved him. What could I have done differently? Was it stopping to put gas in my car? I wished I had done that the day before. But, how was I to know I would be driving back home? Then again, if I were stopped for speeding, it would have taken me even longer to get to the hospital. It seems like from that point on my life has been a lot of careful scheduling and planning. I guess it was to avoid the '*what ifs*' in life".

Chapter Two

Connie knew there were a few loose ends to see to before she moved into the old house, but for all intent and purposes; the house that was once her childhood home was now hers again. After several family phone calls, and one or two face-to-face meetings, it was decided that the family house and property should not be sold, but stay in the family. After all, that's what Edmund Sr. worked so hard for all of his life. And, they were sure the wording in their mother's last Will and Testament expressed the same wishes. The way they went about it was left up to them.

In some families and with some siblings that last request might have been a catalyst for continuous bickering, and even family severances, but not with us. It seemed that Levee and 'Brother' had already decided amongst themselves that neither one of them wanted the full time-responsibility of the property, and sense I was the eldest, it should go to me. *How convenient and forthright of them, I thought.*

Sure, we all agreed it was the best decision, but maybe for different reasons. Olivia was married and had a home of her own. She had to consider her husband, and their soon to come, second child. They lived in the city, but a wife's allegiance was to support the goals and vision that her husband had for their own household. No problem. I totally agree with that. On the other hand;

Brother was not trying to take on any more responsibility that would cramp his free lifestyle, or his finances.

Edmund was almost as frivolous now as he used to be in the past. He was settling down into adulthood but, he sure was taking his time about. At least he's stopped hopping from job to job, and finally decided on something that would hold his interest for a while. It wasn't great money yet, but he was able to keep his bills under control, his apartment and car note paid, and something he was most proud of; he didn't have to borrow money from his sisters anymore. So, there it was! To please the family… Connie had to remember, *I'm the oldest. It's my responsibility.* She had a nice two bedroom apartment in Nashville. But before that, she had to sell her house after her husband was killed. Somehow the decision to stay where she was, (in Nashville) was not an option.
Connie had been away from Georgia for nearly nine years. She came back for a little while after her husband's death, because at that time she couldn't be by herself and bear the burden of grief she was going through. She needed to be with family. Of course, Anthony had family in Nashville, but she wanted my *Mama*.

If it had been just a matter of Anthony's death, that would have been different; maybe something that Connie could have handled (in time). And, though *they* say time heals all wounds, but this wound was a double whammy! Connie was brought up in the church. They all attended St. James CME church. That was her parent's church, Her grandparent's church, and maybe their great grandparent's church. Connie was born in 1937, and there weren't too many *Colored* churches to attend for those living in Stone Quarry, Georgia. They had a choice of the local AM E church, or the Baptists churches on the other side of the tracks. The more prominent larger Baptist congregations were located in the Atlanta area. Her father was on the Deacon board, and her mother was a 'Matron' who later became a Missionary, but more or less to the local community; not the kind that traveled overseas.

I often thought about the stigma associated with my husband's death. It hung over my head, and stayed in my mind. How in the world could he have perished in a nightclub fire? What was he doing there? Who was he with? We attended a church in Nashville on a regular basis. Anthony wasn't one for Wednesday night Bible study, but we went to church most Sundays. When we met in college, Anthony admitted he wasn't much of a church goer. He said he went to his mother's church once in a while, but slacked off once he started college. It probably would have been a good excuse had he been from out of state, but he lived right there in Nashville. I should have gotten a clue right then, but I didn't.

As for me; I was missing home and the fellowship of the saints at my church more than ever. I especially missed my sister, and some of my high school friends. After my first six weeks away from home, and getting settled into college life, I found I started missing some of the very things I thought I would be glad to be free of.

You know—the watchful eye of my parents, the nagging responsibility of being the eldest, and those boring services were at the top of my list. In order to talk to people back home, I had to use the payphone in the Common Hall. The college was only about a three and a half-hour drive from my home, but since I did not own a car at the time, I would have had to take the bus.

I came with the little money my folks and members of my church had given me, but to spend it on a bus ticket back home was silly. The church took up a collection for me the Sunday before I left for college. That was a big blessing, because it was enough money to pay for my books and other school supplies.

My mother and father came to visit me for open–campus Parent Day. I took them to the dorm room I shared with Sylvia Carter. She was from Memphis, Tennessee. I showed them through the small campus and took them to the rooms where my classes were held. Nashville was a little more liberated, or should I say a little less *segregated* back in 1951 than where I came from in Georgia. So, I was able to take them to the local College Malt Shop. It sure was nice to have a place where youth could go and have fun, and not worry about racial prejudices. The local hang out was just a block or two off campus. My parents paid for my lunch, and left me with a small care package which included ten more dollars, and some cards of well wishes from my sister and brother.

Levee's card was a personal handwritten note that said she missed her big sister, and her friend, but it was nice to finally get a bedroom all to herself! She put (ha ha) in parentheses. My parents and I walked back the one block or so to the campus where they had parked, and with a few hugs and kisses they were on their way back home.

I watched the car pull away from the curb. I looked down the road and waved until the car appeared to be nothing more than a mere dot on the horizon. At that moment, I never felt so small and lonely in all of my life. I think that may have been my first feelings of abandonment. I don't know why I felt that way. Everything was good, everything was in order; yet my heart ached as if I had just lost my first love, and maybe I had. I don't mean to say that I lost my parents, but up until that time I only thought of them as parents. But Mom and Pop were real people…people of God who sacrificed their wants and needs because of the love they had for me.

As I ambled across the small campus to my dorm, I thought of the Scripture in the Bible about love.

1 Corinthians Chapter 13

Though I speak with the tongues of men and of angels, and have not charity (love), I am become as sounding brass, or a tinkling cymbal. And though I have the gift of prophecy, and understand all mysteries, and all knowledge; and though I have all faith, so that I could remove mountains, and have not charity, I am nothing.

And though I bestow all my goods to feed the poor, and though I give my body to be burned at, and have not charity, it profits this means nothing.

Charity suffers long and is kind; charity envieth not; charity vaunteth not itself, and is not puffed up, does not behave itself unseemly, seeks not her own, is not easily provoked, thinks no evil; Rejoices not in iniquity, but rejoices in the truth;

Beareth all things, believeth all things, hopeth all things all things, endures all things.

Charity never fails: but whether there be prophecies, they shall fail; whether there be tongues, they shall cease; whether there be knowledge, it shall vanish away. For we know in part, and we prophesy in part. But when that which is perfect is come, then that which is in part shall be done away.

When I was a child, I spake as a child, I understood as a child, I thought as a child: but when I became a man, I put away childish things. For now we see through a glass, darkly; but then face to face: now I know in part; but then shall I know even as I am known.

And now abideth faith, hope, love, these three; but the greatest of these is love.

Reflecting on the words in that text brought back a certain realization about her parents, and herself. Connie knew what she had to do. She would look for a church home while she was attending college. She not only needed love, she needed the fellowship of love too.

Chapter 3

Coming out of her musing, Connie remembered how hot it was by the drop-lets of sweat dripping down from her forehead and trickling down the back of her neck. She didn't know if she wanted to lift up the windows on the lower level of the old house, or to keep them down and turn on the window air-conditioner, but that was down the hall.

The house had two window air conditioners. She bought one for her folks and Olivia bought the other. That of course, had been within the past seven to ten years. Until then, all Mom and Pop used were a couple of window fans, and that *rickety* old floor fan that Pop found at the Salvation Army.

After owning my own house, and now my apartment, I don't see how we all came up in this house without any air-conditioning. I *believe* the summers were just as hot back then as they are now, but I guess being kids we didn't notice it so much.

Anyway, nobody we knew had air-conditioning back then; even most of the white people in town didn't have air-conditioning. I can't remember if the Piggly Wiggly, or the Winn Dixie grocery stores had air-conditioning or not. We mostly went to the store-front markets in our neighborhoods, or the open markets that mainly sold fresh fruits and vegetables. As children we tagged along with our parents, mainly Mama, but waited outside while she shopped for the milk and meat we would need for the week. Those stops were last on the list.

I remember going to shop for groceries was a half day affair, and we knew the purpose of us going along was to help carry the sacks home. However, it did bring us the choice of two candy peppermint sticks, or a nickel. My sister and I always went for the candy, *Brother* went for the nickel; which is why I can't understand why he didn't value money when he got older.

Looking through the eyes of a child, (a grumbling child) I thought I had the heaviest sacks to carry because I was the oldest. But now that I think about it, and get a visual picture of how it really was, I can see my Mother carrying the sacks with the potatoes, or the watermelon in it. Those bags must've been getting heavier and heavier with every few blocks of the nearly one-mile walk home. A wave of guilt came over me again, and I could feel some of my self-righteous indignation dwindling away.

I decided to hoist up the windows for now, and turn on the fan. The other air-conditioner was upstairs in what was now used as a guest bedroom. It was the room on the front of the house, and it got more of the sun because the few trees that were out front were further away from the house then the trees that were in the back. Actually it's because the sun came in on the front of the house. Levee and I shared one of the bedrooms on the backside of the house, and Edmund had the other. Those rooms caught the cool of the evening, and the shade from the

Oak and Walnut trees during the day. Just letting the window fan draw in the night air kept the rooms in the back cool, and if we placed another fan at the bedroom door, it drew the cool air all the way down the hallway. The house originally had the three bedrooms upstairs and the one bathroom in the hall, but the family who owned the house before us must have added the extra bedroom downstairs. They also added that small bathroom adjacent to the kitchen area.

When we got older our dad told us it looked to him like that at one time the extra bathroom downstairs was once part of a big walk-in pantry. The last owners must have taken away from the pantry in order to add on the extra bathroom. If they had two or three small children, which most families did back then, the added downstairs bathroom probably kept the kids from coming through the house messing up the foyer and living room. I remember Pop saying; "because of that, '*Mister Boss Man*' charged me extra rent for this house." Colored folks back then weren't supposed to have homes that nice. Mom was the house cleaning, cook, and babysitter for the Mayor and his wife. Those are my words. Back then they just called her the *maid*.

And since our family had the larger house; when pastors came from out of town to preach a revival arrangements were made between the pastor and my Dad for them to stay with us. Not in the sense that our home was used as a hotel for visiting pastors (and their wives), but there was nowhere else for them to stay back then. They surly couldn't stay in any hotels in Atlanta. So, the blessing of the Lord was that we could offer them a place to stay. It was the favor of God that we were blessed to have the house anyway.

I know that to be true because it was favor that got it in my parent's hands in the first place. It all happened when the Mayor found out about the overcharging for rent, he told his wife to increase my mother's pay by that same amount of money we were being overcharged. But, instead of Mom bringing the money home for us to live on, she and Pop along with the mayor's wife came up with a secret savings plan.

Mrs. Styles told the bank she was setting aside a special savings account for a niece of hers to surprise her with college money when she graduated from High school. All I know is that by the time I graduated high school, and Mama had helped to raise the Mayor's kids; my parents had saved enough money to pay the balance of the mortgage in cash. Come to find out, Pop was putting back a little money every week too. Except, his money did not go to the bank. It was in the box springs of their old mattress set.

They waited all those years, because Pop had become aware of a clause in the contract that gave them the first right to purchase the property should it ever go up for sale. I guess way back then in the early forties, the real estate company never expected that a black man could get his hands on that much money anyway. I believe they are still puzzled until this very today as to where all the money came from. Mrs. Styles closed her *so called* special savings account in 1954. I was about seventeen years old and had one more year before I graduated high school. Her husband was no longer the Mayor, but Mom still worked for them.

Mr. *Boss Man,* and Company overcharged my Dad about $60.00 a month. Between his job at the quarry, and doing handyman's work he managed to pay the rent. The twelve years of the secret savings account had accumulated $8,640.00. The account drew 5% interest, which put the total monies close to $9,000.00. In that same amount of time, my dad had managed to save $5,760.00. This all happened with him just setting aside $10.00 a week for almost twelve years. Between the both of them, my parents had saved $14,832.00. This was unbelievable, and unheard of, considering the struggle that 'Blacks' were going through in those days

---

Connie returned to the kitchen. She stood in the middle of the floor with both hands on her hips. There really wasn't much to do. The times she did meet face to face with Edmond and Olivia, they met at the house to sort through things they wanted to keep, and to discard the things that were no longer needed. If there was a certain pot, or skillet that held memories for one of them, they would keep that item out of the Goodwill/Salvation Army pile. Being grown now, most of them, except for Edmund had their own households and whatever it took to make them run smoothly. Even so, many things were left *as-is* until they made a final decision of who would get full ownership of the Webster family home.

Connie started in the kitchen with the top cabinet at the far end of the stove. It was pretty much cleared of its past condiments and seasonings. There was plenty of room for what she would bring from her apartment this coming week. The next two cabinets that use to hold can goods and such were empty. A lot of that went to Edmund. He wasn't a great cook, but having the cans of vegetables, bags of cornmeal and flour, rice, beans and other *like* staples in his cupboard would hopefully inspire him to eat *in* more, rather than going out for meals.

The short cabinet over the sink, and the large one next to it held coffee cups, glassware, and the everyday dishes. Those went to Levee. She was the one with the husband and children. Mother's good dishes were in the China cabinet in the dining room. The family decided that those should be passed down to *the eldest*. The dishes were vastly becoming a family heirloom. They first belonged to Connie's grandmother. The set was given to her as a wedding gift from the family she worked for. Now, the china has been passed on to a third generation. The set of dishes didn't have a long history, but at least it had a good start.

After that, Connie pulled out the long drawer at the end of the counter above the bottom cabinet. It was what they called the *catch-all* drawer. The family didn't worry about going through that particular drawer when they did their sweep-*threw*. That was left for Connie to do on her arrival. The drawer held things one often used, but not enough times for them to merit a separate drawer, or storing place of their own. Connie pushed aside a few cutlery knives, an extension cord, a couple of folded drying towels for the dishes, a pack of matches, and then she ran across a small stack of index cards wrapped in a rubber band. She took the index cards out, and pushed the drawer shut with the side of her hip.

Seeing that the cards had handwriting on them; she moved to the kitchen table and pulled out a chair. They were recipes. What? She never remembered her mother using recipes. Looking closer at the writing caused her to take in an unexpected deep breath. She was very young at the time, maybe nine or ten when her grandmother passed away, but she was sure this was *Granny's* handwriting. Browsing through a couple of the index cards Connie certainly remembered enjoying some of these meals and desserts. Each card she read brought back a particular childhood memory.

Hot Water Cornbread

2 cups plain yellow cornmeal

¼ cup minced onion

Bacon bits (freshly fried/jar)   optional

1 cup vegetable oil or shortening

Boiling water

Mix meal, onion and bacon bits. Slowly add boiling water until mixture thickens enough to form into patties when shaped by hand. Heat oil in cast iron skillet. Place cornbread patties in heated oil for 1-1½ minutes, or until edges are browned. Turn patties over and brown on the other side. Remove and place on paper towel to drain and soak up excess grease. Serve hot.

Chapter 4

Connie sat for a while and reminisced about the warm family moments of carefree childhood, and then she got up from the table to see what else the *'catch all'* drawer held.

She found a small cardboard box in the little pantry area and began to put things in it to take to the Salvation Army Outlet. The refrigerator was working, and the freezer had two trays of ice cubes in it, but little of anything else. Connie knew she would be working for another hour or so, and she would want something else to drink besides water.

She looked at the containers lined against the back of the kitchen counter. Good! The ones that were for flour and coffee were empty, (the family disposed of their contents at the last family walk through). But, the containers marked 'sugar' and 'tea' still held those items. Connie took four teabags from the container and looked in one of the top cabinets for the glass pitcher. She found her mother's aluminum teapot in the bottom cabinet near the stove. She rinsed the teapot and filled it with water. In the next two or three steps she was on her way to making a good old-fashioned pitcher of iced tea. She knew that the teakettle would sound its whistle when the water boiled. In the meantime, she would browse the pantry shelf for any can goods that were left, and maybe some cleaning supplies.

Connie stood reading the label on the back of the Pine-Sol bottle, when the foreign sound of the whistling tea-kettle startled her. She ran to turn the burner off, and then put the teabags in the heavy glass pitcher. While the boiled water cooled down, Connie turned her attention toward the dining room. She no sooner pulled open the center drawer to the buffet cabinet, when the blaring ring tone of the telephone sounded. What in the world! It rang a second time. She guessed Edmund must have done his part after all. She picked up the receiver and barely got out her "hello", when Edmunds voice came through the other end loud and clear.

"Good afternoon Madam, could you please tell me if the lady of the house is at home"? "*Brother*, you are always joking. But, you are coming through loud and clear. Thank you."

"Hey Sis, sorry I couldn't get over there. I was trying to get this phone service on for you, but I ran into a couple of snags."

"Snags, why? Don't tell me you ran out of money."

"Very funny smarty-pants, as a matter of fact, the problem was with you."

"What?"

"What I meant was the problem wasn't with you. I mean the problem was with your name. I didn't know how you wanted your name listed in the telephone directory. It could have been listed as Constance Webster, or listed as Constance Webster-Black."

"Gosh, I didn't think about that."
"Wow! You mean to tell me that my older, big *city* living, sister didn't think of an important detail like that?"

"Cut it out *Brother*. So, what did you end up doing?"
"Well, I couldn't get in touch with you of course, to ask you how you wanted it listed, so I did the only thing that made sense to me."

Connie was afraid to ask what that was, so she waited for him to finish; hoping for the best. When brother didn't hear anything during the pause, he continued.

"I hyphenated your last names. I know how *Modern-day* women do things now. So, I had it listed as Constance Webster-Black."
Connie thought for a couple of seconds before she began to speak.

"Well, I guess that's okay. I usually use my married name on everything, but that was back in Nashville. Now that I'm back home, most of my friends and relatives know me by Connie Webster anyway. You did good Edmund.
You did Good!"

"Hey, you said a couple of snags. What was the other one?"
"Oh yeah! I guess the new thing with getting phone numbers now is that you have a few numbers to choose from. The last phone number used for this last name and address had been given out to someone else over a year ago, so I chose a new number. It's very close to the number that Pop and Mom had. And, check this out. It's only one digit off. Do you have something to write it down on?"

The center drawer to the buffet was still open and Connie stretched the coiled cord to reach for the pad of writing paper and ink pen that was lying in view. She wrote the telephone number down; 404-837-8370.

Edmund said he would have to get on to work, but he would drop by in the morning. Connie thanked him, and put the receiver back on the cradle. She rewrote the number at the bottom of the pad, and tore it off to put in her purse. With all the other things on her mind, although the new number was so close to the one her folks used to have, she knew it would take a couple of days before she could remember it by heart.

Before heading back to her folk's bedroom, she retrieved the small box she had gotten from the pantry. Connie went to the kitchen and made the pitcher of iced tea. She poured the warm water over the teabags, and covered the top with a saucer to let the tea steep. After about five minutes she planned to return to the teabags. Connie sweetened the tea while it was still warm. She used half measures each of cane sugar and the honey. She wouldn't add lemon to the tea until after it had chilled.

Chapter 5

Connie had still not decided if she was going to take her parent's bedroom for her own, or use her old one upstairs. She contemplated on how she would feel–on how it would affect her grief. The move back to her parent's home was stirring enough. She had managed well enough the last few times she was here, but then again, all of her siblings were here too. This time she had to go it alone. This time it was just her and her memories; just her and her streams of unsettled grief.

Connie raised her shoulders up and down, and took in a couple of deep breaths. She opened the door at the end of the hallway, and stepped inside the room. Her eyes fell on each of the neat and orderly items kept in her parent's bedroom. The bureau against the small wall over her left shoulder, the closed door that led to the walk-in closet next to that; the French-pane glass door that led out to the side porch, the Hi-Boy dresser, and the double poster bed in front of her. There was a nightstand next to the bed, and a two legged full length dressing mirror that tilted in its frame, next to that.

Connie had to smile when the vision of her mother checking, and double checking her image in the long floor mirror came to mind. Especially, when she would turn her back to the mirror and look over her shoulder to see if anything was hiked-up, or out of order in the back.

"It may seem like an unnecessary thing, her mother would say, *however a woman should look just as decent coming as she does walking away!"* Then she would lower her chin to her neck, raised her eyebrows with an expression that said… *And you know what I mean!* Actually, at the time we girls weren't quite sure what she meant, maybe that's because we were not as well-endowed as Mama was. But, as we became older it became an automatic thing for us to do before leaving our bedrooms, or the house.

That fond memory seemed to take the edge off of Connie's feelings. On the wall next to that was a round Mahogany table and a tufted Wing-back chair.

Years ago a rocking chair sat where the tufted chair was now, but about ten years ago when Mrs. Styles was refurnishing a few of the rooms in her home, she asked Mama if she wanted a few of her things. My mother told her yes. The way she figured it was; no use letting Mrs. Styles donate the items to the Salvation Army, and then go down to the thrift store to pay money for the same thing she could get for free. After a little bit, Mom gave the rocking chair to the Levee when she got married. Knowing one thing would follow another, she probably knew that it would be just a short while before the old rocking chair would come in handy.

By now the issue was settled. Connie knew she would take her parent's old bedroom for her own.

Anyway, what sense does it make in trying to haul and rearrange all that heavy furniture up the stairs? She would have some help, but no use trying to make workhorses out of everyone. Connie had already scaled down her household possessions when she moved from the house she and her late husband lived in, to the two-bedroom apartment where she now resided for the past four years. When it became apparent that the move back to Stone Quarry was inevitable, she invited Anthony's family to come to her home first for the private moving sale she was having.

After that, she invited some of the folks from the church she attended. Connie kept her personal clothes and her books. She sold most of her furniture. She wouldn't need her bedroom set, there were more than enough bedroom sets at her folks house. She had sold most everything she knew she didn't need, or what she could get again later. She would not have a steady income for a while, so the extra money would come in handy.

When she moved from the house to the apartment, Connie was able to save about a fourth of her paycheck. Not having the full expense of the home and property taxes on her budget was a big help. She always believed in putting a little back for emergency sake. Connie guessed she learned that from her parents. All the rage now was about getting a credit card. It was 1970, and the media was giving great attention to the credit card industry. Everywhere you went, retailers were giving a 10% off discount if you signed up for their in-store credit card, or for what they called a major credit card.

Connie was so glad she was never tempted to own

one. Everything she had, she owned out right; even her car. She brought a 1967 Chevy Impala a few years ago. Connie didn't have all the money to pay for the car at that time, but the amount that she did have brought the price down, and she borrowed the balance from her credit union; not a bank. Eighteen months later, she owned her own car. Paying off the vehicle in eighteen months gave her an excellent credit rating.

Connie kept her large living room mirror, her sofa table, a room divider, a few modern table lamps and something she had become used to using–her microwave oven. She didn't use it to cook meals, but it was handy for warming up leftovers, and heating water for a cup of tea, or instant coffee. When her spirits were up, she would hum, or sing some of her favorite songs like: *'Sugar Pie Honey Bunch'* or This Magic Moment'.

She was excited about the move, but her spirit did sway back and forth a little. This only added to her grief. She was very fond of her Mother-in-law, and had made close friends with some of her co-workers. Those acquaintances had been two of the steady factors in her life since the death of her husband, and now even that rug was being snatched out from under her.

Whenever that feeling of forlornness came over her, Connie would be reminded of the way she felt that day at college when she stood watching her parent's car travel down the road and fade into nothingness. Then her heart would sing a different tune like; 'Sitting on the Dock of the Bay', or Band of Gold'. It was during those moments she asked…*When will love stick around for me? Will I ever feel loved again?*

Then a still quiet voice would whisper in her heart, *"Here I Am"*, and she knew it was the Lord.

———

Moving day was easy. Edmund drove up to Nashville in a pickup truck with one of his friends, George. George and his wife, along with Edmund owned a little store-front flea market. Edmund had one of those Volkswagen vans, and George owned the pickup truck. I had boxed up all of my clothes, books, and what little glassware and knickknacks I was planning on taking with me. The guys crammed everything they could into my '67 Chevy Impala, leaving me a peep hole through the back window, and they put everything else in the pickup truck.

I had already said my goodbyes to the *Blacks,* and promised to call my in-laws when I got settled, and my phone service was turned on. Mama Black wanted to know if I needed to take along some of the mementoes she had saved of Anthony's years at home. She thought that would be something to remind me of my late husband. But what she didn't know was, I was trying to *forget* some of those memories—not take them along with me.

Notwithstanding, as it was, the little things I tried to ignore about my marriage to Anthony, somehow seeped back into my conscious, and soon foggy things became crystal clear.

41

One of those remembrances was when I found out Anthony was secretly going downtown to the free-clinic. I was so naïve, I kept trying to do everything I could to entice my husband to make love to me. I had no idea of what I was doing wrong. I sort of mentioned it to my mother-in-law, but the only advice I got from her was to be patient; sometimes men go through these down times. I had nothing to worry about.

I might have had nothing to worry about, but I also had no idea what she was talking about, or what she meant by *downtime. He was in his twenties.* I was glad I didn't force the issue any further with her, or with him. Come to find out, he was being treated for one of those sexually transmitted diseases. I don't know if it was for Syphilis, Gonorrhea, or the Clapp, but I was (and still am) grateful to God that Anthony thought enough of me as a Christian woman not to pass residue from his infidelity on to me.

Because Connie had previously decided where everything was to be placed, she was pretty much moved in by the end of the day on Friday. There were only a couple of families Connie knew from childhood days, who still lived on Stone Quarry Road. There used to be four Caucasian families, and three Negro families on that strip of road. Now, only two of the Caucasian families were still there, and the other houses that were left were now occupied by other Black families.

Connie had to laugh to herself. Now that things had changed she was thankful for the "Nosy" neighbors—at least for the two families she had known before she lived in Nashville. Stone Quarry Road only had houses on one side of the street. Although the houses sat a ways back from the road, the front of those houses faced the railroad tracks.

The city put a paved road down that street around 1965. Until that time, the concrete roads only ran throughout the downtown area. Because the freight train hauled rocks from the quarry, the workers would stand across from the Sheriff's station to catch a train ride up to the mountain early in the morning. After their 10 to 12 hour work day was over, they would ride the loaded freight train back down to the middle of town. It became such a popular pick up and, drop off point that the railroad company added a small passenger train to its line. That allowed businessmen and 'White' families who had to ride into Atlanta board a separate coach away from the working class. Of course the small added coach offered better comfort, and those who could afford it did not squirm over the higher price.

Chapter 6

Edmund, Olivia and her husband Earl helped Connie to set the house in order. After several hours of work they got hungry. While the men went out to get Colonial Sanders chicken and fixings for dinner; Connie and Olivia washed the needed plates, glasses, and silverware for the meal. When the two sisters were talking, Connie began to know how much her sister Levee missed their mother.

Levee and Edmund never left Stone Quarry, so they saw their parents all the time. I was only a few years apart in age from my siblings, but these few moments alone with my sister made me more sensitive to the grief she and my brother must be going through. It made me wonder how I would feel if I had stayed, and had the chance to see Mom at least three or four times a week, or talked with her every day on the phone? Now even a deeper sorrow panged my heart, but this time it was for them.

Connie looked around the table at her family. She felt a wave of comfort and peace enter her spirit. So, this is what *home* was going to feel like. The chime of the front doorbell interrupted her musing, and also bought a startling look to those around the table, as if to say; *"who could that be"?* Connie wiped her hands on one of the paper napkins the guys threw in the take-out bag, and rose from the table. It was late August, and Day-light Savings Time, so even at nine o'clock in the evening it was not quite dark. Still, Edmund pushed his chair back from the table and followed his sister to the door.

The front door was shut, and the screen was hooked. Edmund didn't say anything, at least not with his lips, but Connie caught the look in his eyes, and the scowl on his face that said; *'this girls been used to the big city living for so long, I guess she forgot it's unusual for us Southerners to lock our doors'*. Connie opened the door to find Mrs. Miller standing on the front porch. What a surprise.

"Good evening, the elderly woman said, welcome back home Constance." Connie was speechless. Not only had Sister Ida Mae Miller lived two doors down from her Mama all these years; she was one of her mother's best friends. Neither she, nor Edmund said anything for a moment, so Mrs. Miller chimed in again.
"I hope I'm not interrupting anything. I know how tired you and your family must be from all that moving back home you've been doing" Her teenage grandson was standing slightly behind her and just to her left. "Oh. Miss Constance you don't know my grandson? This is Thomas, Eli's boy. He comes to visit us most every summer, but you wouldn't know that since you've been gone all these years. He'll be going back home when school starts back after Labor Day." Connie waited for her chance to get a word in edge-wise. It all came back to her now. She remembered how much of a talker Mrs. Miller was.

"Hello Mrs. Miller. It's good to see you again. Forgive my manners. Won't you and your grandson come on in?"

Mrs. Miller raised the brown paper bag in the air that she was holding in her hand, and gave it to Connie.

"Oh, not right now dearie. We'll have plenty of time to visit later on. I just wanted to say *welcome* back to the neighborhood, and to do the neighborly thing and drop by. I baked you one of my pound cakes. Since your sister and brother are here, you can cut them a nice size slice too."

"Thank you so much Mrs. Miller that was very nice of you to do. *Umm*, it smells so good."

Connie stepped closer to the elderly lady and gave her a kiss on the cheek.

"Are you sure you won't come in fora few minutes? We would love to have you." Connie felt a prodding knuckle in the center of her back as Edmund cleared his throat. "No thank you. It's getting kind of late, and I'm sure Thomas wants to hang outside a little while longer with his friends; especially that little gal named Nor..."

"Grandma!" He cut her off before she could finish the girl's name.

"O *boy,* nobody cares 'bout that little ole gal you call yourself *lacking*."

Thomas already had taken hold of his grandmother's elbow turning her away from the door to head down the porch steps. Edmund took the package from Connie's hands. He could still feel the warmth of the cake coming through the plate it sat on in the wrapped brown paper bag.

47

Before closing the door Connie looked to see that Thomas and his grandmother had neared the end of the stoned-paved driveway and were evidently in deep conversation. She could only suppose it was about the name that almost slipped from Mrs. Miller's lips. A hearty smile encompassed her face, and then suddenly it dropped when she remembered that her brother had made off with the pound cake. By the time she got to the kitchen, the pound cake was under attack.

Connie thanked her sisters, her brother-in-law Earl, and Edmund again for all the moving help they had given her. All were sent home with ample slices of pound cake, and Connie refrigerated what was left of the fried chicken. She still had a few boxes to unpack on tomorrow, and hopefully would get to the grocery store. But the day had been long and tiresome. She was very exhausted, and needed to go to bed.

Edmund had offered to spend the night, but Connie convinced him she would be just fine. It was very late, so she would have to put the call to her mother-in-law on the "*to do*" list for tomorrow. The evening temperature had dropped some, but not much from its daytime high. She suspected the temperature was still in the mid-80s.

Connie made sure all the windows were down, and the house was secure. She knew it would take some time before she was used to living in a home again. She had become so use to her second-floor apartment in Nashville. She didn't have to worry about ground-level intruders. Although she had heard on the news of several apartment break-ins, none of those had happened in the

part of town where she lived. And, the few she did hear of
happened
at ground level where it was easy for intruders to come
in through an unlocked window.

There were two bathrooms in the house. There was
the one off the kitchen; which only had a wash-up sink
in it, and the one upstairs which was a full bathroom.
It was very large, almost the size of a small bedroom. If
Connie was going to sleep in her new bedroom tonight,
she might as well washed up in the bathroom on the first
floor. She looked through the drawer and found a pair of
her summer PJs. She opened the walk-in closet, pulled
out her slippers and a light robe tossing them on the bed
with the PJs.

She stood near the big four-poster bed, and looked
around the room. *'You can do this'*, she thought to
herself,' *You can do this'*. Connie set on the edge of the
bed. *Maybe I'm not quite ready for this. Maybe I should
have asked Edmund to spend the night.* "No, she spoke
out loud. Then what about the next night, and the next
night after that?"

She popped up off of the bed, and gathered the
garments in her hand. Connie pushed her feet into her
slippers, and headed down the hall. The kitchen light was
still on, but she would have to rectify that. She couldn't
let a100 watt bulb burn all night long and run up the
electric bill. She would have to add a night-light to her
"*to do*" list.

Once in the bathroom, Connie realized there were

only two hand towels hanging on the towel bar. After all, this bathroom had only been for quick uses. She would have to bring in one of those little decorative tables she had, and arrange one of Mama's set of guest towels on it.

She also thought she would sit a basket on the small shelf of table, and roll up some more bath towels in it; and she might put some of those little decorative soaps in it too.

Connie headed up the stairs. She could already feel how much warmer the upstairs was as she ascended the steps. The air was stuffy. She got a large bath towel from the linen closet built inside the huge bathroom. A second thought entered her mind. Maybe this was the feeling of security she needed for tonight. Connie plodded down the hallway to the front guest bedroom, flipped on the light switch, and went to the air-conditioner mounted in one of the front windows. She turned the knob on, and the motor revved up. Connie waited a minute to see if the cool air would escape from its grill. T hank the Lord! Cool air was on its way. She pushed the reset button, and left the fan on high.

By the time she finished her shower, hopefully the room would be cool. Connie really wanted to soak in the bathtub, knowing that by tomorrow morning her body would be feeling the soreness from using muscles she had not used for a while. But, she also knew that soaking in that relaxing, warm water could cause her to unwind too much, and she didn't want to end up nodding off while taking a bath.

The front bedroom was more than cool enough when Connie returned from the bathroom. She turned the temperature from 65° up to 72°. She turned the fan down to the medium setting, and jumped into bed. She sank down under the familiar quilt set that once belonged to her grandmother. It was handed down to her mother, and now it belonged to her.

Her head nestled in the goose-down feather pillow as her eyes gave way to much needed sleep. Somewhere between coziness and actually falling asleep, she heard the distant whistle of the night train and the rumble of its wheels, as they bumped against the wooden rails. Childhood memories of lying in bed listening to that train seeped into her thoughts, and she couldn't tell if she was already dreaming, or if she was actually hearing the train whistle.

Dozing off, something Levee said to her that evening came back into her hearing. It was about Otis. "Oh yes, she said, won't it be exciting to see Otis again? I know he'll be glad to see you."

Chapter 7

Saturday morning came, and Connie was sure it was going to be a scorcher. With that in mind, she set out to take care of the things on her "*to do*" list that would take her away from the house. She got up early; maybe a bit too early, but she was still used to getting up early for work. After all, it had only been two weeks since she left her job.

Before she left the house, Connie called her mother-in-law to let her know that everything had gone smoothly, and she was on her way out to purchase a few items for the house. Connie waited until Mrs. Black got an ink pen and a piece of paper so she could give her mother-in-law her new telephone number. They exchanged a few more thoughts, and she said she would be calling her again very soon.

Connie still didn't feel comfortable about leaving any downstairs windows hoisted-up, or doors unlocked. The best thing she could think of to do right now, was to turn on the window air-conditioner in her folks–in her bedroom, and set the old floor fan at the open doorway to draw the cool air down the hall. Hopefully by doing that it would travel into the open living and dining room areas. She didn't want to keep the air-conditioner running too long. Connie knew she was being frugal when it came to using what monies she had to spend, but she no longer had a paycheck coming in twice a month, and the funny thing about that was; she didn't have 'find a job' on her "*to do*" list. That wasn't anything to worry about at that moment she guessed, and she didn't know why she felt that way.

Connie checked the gas gauge on the dashboard. She had not used the car since her drive from Nashville on Friday, and the needle was registering just under one-forth of a tank. The Winn Dixie grocery store was in the plaza only a few blocks away. She wasn't worried that her Chevy Impala would run out of gas going that short a distance. Connie made the move from Nashville with one full tank of gas, but she also paid for the gas in the pickup truck.
She was glad her father-in-law knew something about cars.

He volunteered to go car shopping with her, and it was on his suggestion that she ended up with the Chevy Impala. It was new when she bought it, and he told her it was a solid car, and it ought to last her for many a year. All she had to do was to keep it maintained at least twice a year; if it needed it, or not, and it would keep her worry free.

On her first day out, Connie didn't expect to run into anyone she knew. However, she recognized the cashier at the check-out counter. Elaine was one grade ahead of her in school, but was in the same Home Economics class. Since Home Economics was an *Elective*, the three high school grades shared the same class hour. The schools were not integrated back then, so most of the *Electives* in the *'Black'* schools were taught by one teacher for the Jr. High grades (seven through nine), and the High School grades ten through twelve.

Connie checked her items out at Elaine's counter. She said she was married, and had three children. The oldest one was going to begin the fourth grade this year. She went on to say she would probably see me in church on Sunday, and mentioned again how sorry she was when she heard about my husband's death. The way she said it seemed like she was fishing for some new news about my attachments. I wasn't about to accommodate her. I left the checkout counter with my two bags in hand saying how nice it was to see her again. Besides; even if I had *new news* in my life; which I didn't, I surely wasn't going to share that with her.

Connie put away the groceries, and the few other toiletry items she picked up from Mays Drugstore. She unpacked the last two boxes that were marked, 'Kitchen', and 'Pantry'. It was just about noon, and the temperature was on the rise. She decided to take a short break and fix a sandwich for lunch. Then she had in mind to tackle the remaining suitcases in the bedroom that held most of her wardrobe. She had Edmund to leave the box with the books in it in the middle of the living room floor. There were so many other things that needed to be moved and arranged in the house yesterday; that Connie had to take advantage of the male help while it was available.

Connie knew she wanted a small bookshelf in the bedroom. She thought about getting the one that was upstairs in her old bedroom. Her plan was to use the living room as the main room for accepting company, and entertaining, so she didn't want a bookshelf in there. Then again, the small Parlor would make an excellent place for a study. Well, maybe not a study, but a nice room to sit in and read. It was cozy and comfortable. Only, during the summer months the room got much too warm in the day, but come this fall and winter (she thought), the warmth coming through the window would be nice and inviting.

Connie poured a glass of sweet tea to have with her sandwich. Her mind was still pondering over where the books would go, and if she needed the bookshelf from upstairs, when the telephone rang. It was Edmund. He said he had called earlier but didn't get an answer. She told him she went to the grocery store and stopped to put gas in the car on the way back home.

Edmund said he called to see how she made it through the night, and also wanted to know if there was anything else she needed for him to do. The bookshelf was fresh on her mind. He said George and Joanna could handle the flea market for the rest of the day. He was coming over to cut the grass, but if she still needed his help inside, he wanted to get that done first.

Connie hung up the phone and returned to her lunch. She thought that was so sweet of her brother to ask how she *made it through the night;* she hadn't even thought about the grass. *Umm,* maybe my little brother has matured a little after all. Connie smiled to herself, "*I guess people stopped calling him 'Little Eddie' years ago.*

I guess I'll have to catch up." Connie went upstairs to clear off the bookshelf. There really wasn't anything much in the way of substantial reading material left. When she left for college, she took her yearbook, her Bible, and a few of the novels she still wanted to read. She left most of the other books behind for Olivia. From the looks of things, Levee had left most of them behind too.

Chapter 8

Edmunds voice came bellowing through the house.

"Sis. Hey Sis. Where are?"

Connie went to the bedroom door and leaned her head out into the hallway.

"I'm up here in my old room."

Edmund mounted the steps two at a time.

"Wow! Is it ever hot up here?"

Connie had not noticed that she was trickling with sweat. She went to the closet in the hallway, and grabbed a face cloth. She wiped her face and the back of her neck with the pink washcloth, and then stuffed it in the pocket of her Bermuda shorts. She told her brother she was still trying to decide where she wanted the bookshelf to go.

He told her he thought the Parlor was a good idea, mainly because the television set was in the living room. Her bedroom was an okay idea he said, but those who wanted to sit and browse through a book would have to go into her private bedroom to get it.

Again, Connie thought, *"Wow!"* What's going on with my little brother? It also reminded her how proud their parents were of the Parlor; not in a haughty kind of way, but humble.

Their parents sacrificed a great deal for family and for the church. They didn't look for anything in return, but God always supplied their every need. Most of the furnishings in the Parlor were either donated, or

59

purchased at the thrift store. That included the Victorian-style Settee sofa, and matching chairs, the Baldwin piano, and the lavish throw rug. The room also housed a grandfather clock.

The old slender floor radio was in one corner of the rectangle shaped room, and a Maplewood Cairo cabinet stood in the other. It was clearly a room designed for sitting and meditating while someone played the piano, or to listen to the radio; which by the way still worked. Yes, the bookcase will work just fine in the Parlor!

Edmund went out to cut the grass, and Connie loaded the books in a small box, and carried them downstairs. She agreed that the small bookcase would look nice on the left wall as you entered the room. The upright piano was in the center of the wall. Before he went out, they moved the piano down about three more feet from where it originally sat. After Edmund left, Connie moved the floor lamp from the corner closer in to the piano, and the small bookcase fit perfectly in that niched out space. She looked around the room. Except for the bookcase she added today, and the freestanding radio in its walnut encasement, which had been moved to the Parlor in 1952 when they got their first television set the room had not changed much.

Connie was fifteen years old when the Styles' were purchasing a brand new color TV manufactured by RCA. They asked Mom and Dad if they would like to have one of their old black and white TV sets. There again, we had something that most 'Black' families didn't own. Come to think of it, most of the 'Whites' we knew didn't own TV sets either. But, those blessings came by the way of favor–not finance.

The afternoon temperature was hot. It was well over 90°. Connie took a tall glass of sweet tea out to her brother who had worked his way around to mowing the back yard. She invited Edmund to stay for dinner. There were several pieces of the takeout chicken left from the night before; so by adding some vegetables and a starch, it wouldn't take much to make a good hearty meal.

Connie turned on the window air-conditioner in her bedroom, and did her little trick with the arranging of the two fans to draw all the coolness down the hallway towards the open living/dining room area. She closed the Parlor door to prevent any of the cool air from seeping into a spaces not needed. Connie prepared a tossed salad for the vegetable to go along with the fried chicken, and then boiled some corn on the cob. For dessert they could have a scoop of ice cream to go with a nice slice of Mrs. Miller's pound cake. She and Edmund talked over dinner discussing *this* and *that*. She assured him he didn't have to spend the night with her that she would be all right.

As the evening drew near, Connie twiddled and fiddled around the house. She did some needed dusting, and placed some of the remaining knickknacks in their places. When she had finished in the front part of the house, she checked the locks on the front door, and went into the Parlor to turn on the table lamp sitting on the stand in front of the window.

Thinking twice about it, she turned it off, and walked across the room to turn on the floor lamp near the piano instead. For one, that lamp had a 60 watt bulb in it, not a 75 watt bulb like the lamp on the table. And secondly, the bright light might give the wrong suggestion that: *'we're still up. Come on in for a visit.'* Connie did not know why this sudden feeling of being anti-social was developing in her character. *"Maybe"*, she thought, *"I just don't want people asking me questions about what happened between me and my husband, and... why I have no children."*

Connie turned out to the kitchen light, and clicked on the night light she'd brought earlier at the drugstore. Although she was coming back through the kitchen to sponge off in the small bathroom, she surely didn't want a 100 watt bulb blazing her every move. She turned off the other fan that drew the air from the open dining room area into the kitchen, and went to her bedroom. Connie turned the fan setting on the air conditioner to medium, and darted down the hallway to take a quick wash up. She grabbed one of the rolled up towels from the decorative basket to dry off. Standing there, Connie wondered if it would be possible to reconstruct the walls between the bathroom and her bedroom in order to create an easy access between the two.

She began to thumb through her wardrobe again. She emptied her suitcases, and the two boxes that held her handbags and shoes, she was already thinking about what she would wear to church on Sunday. Her wardrobe didn't hold much of what she thought people were going to expect a young Baptist widow in her early thirties to wear. But she knew she had very conservative clothes, no matter what the *old fogies* thought.

It wasn't that she didn't dress decently where she attended church in Nashville, it was just that church wasn't so strict on traditional dress codes. As a matter-of-fact, that particular congregation had a heavy population of youth and young adults; probably because of the college, and the influx of young folks waiting for their break to make it big in the music industry.

That was just a few years back when they were in the mid-to late 1960s with the introduction of the miniskirt. *Afro* hairstyles, and stacked platform shoes were the height of fashion. Of course, the church tried its best to filter what the young adults, (especially the females) wore, but it was the sign of the times. We had the older church members who were fifty years plus, and the teenage through the twenty-nine, and a group of thirty year olds. Then, there was that age group that I fell in. Some of the thirty to forty years old were parents, and had a much safer guideline in how they dressed; you know–being parents and all. They had a certain image to portray, but the singles, at least the single ladies of my age group had tougher fashions decisions to make. We were too mature to be called young, and not old enough that they expected us to dress like the *'church Mothers'*.

In the way of fashion, there wasn't too much that appealed to me at that time anyway. I had a certain style in mind, and I would have been hard pressed to find it being sold in any of the local department store. Since I worked as a receptionist in an office, and was married when I started the job, I ended up sewing some of my clothes (thank goodness I could sew), and to help with the budget, the others I got from thrift shops, or the Goodwill stores. It wasn't that I was so cheap. I just wanted to dress in a business, conservative type of style that said something about the woman I was. And, the miniskirt just didn't do the trick.

Connie continued to search through her wardrobe. She selected an unlined off-white two-piece suit. She got out a sleeveless navy shell blouse, and her navy blue leather pumps. Connie laid the ensemble across the foot of the bed, and stood back a ways to see if that was the look she was going for. She didn't want to look so patriotic, but the only other 'pop of color' she could think of to wear with the outfit was red.

She went to the yet to be unpacked small box on the dresser, and searched through its contents. She found the red clip earrings and necklace set her mother-in-law gave to her two Christmas' ago. Connie laid the jewelry next to the suit. Everything looked fine. She had not worn that suit sense Mother's Day service at her old church. She was sure the suit would fit her, but just as a precaution, she undid the skirt from the hanger.

She put her feet in the opening and pulled the skirt up over her hips. It fit just perfectly. Considering the foundations she would have on tomorrow, everything would fall in to place smoothly. Connie thought, *"Better safe than sorry"*. She cleared the bed, moving all the accessories to the Queen Ann chair. She rehung the suit and shell in the front of the closet for easy reaching.

Just before she turned out the light, Connie turned to look at the person in the mirror. The reflection was her all right, but where was the joy? She turned off the lamp and sat on the edge of the bed. She prayed to the Lord for His protection, His solace, His guidance, and His love. She stood to her feet and pulled back the quilted spread, the blanket, and folded them over to the end of the bed.

Connie crawled into bed reciting the Lord's Prayer to herself. She was trying not to think of her Mom and Dad. This was their room; there haven. "Now Lord, she prayed, please make it mine." Nestling her head in the feather pillows, she drifted off to sleep, and again she heard her sister's voice say, *"He'll be glad to see you again. He'll be glad to see you."*

Fresh Turnip Greens

3 pounds crisp Turnip greens
4 cups water
2 teaspoons salt
1 teaspoon pepper
¼ pound thinly sliced fatback (salt pork)

Wash and pick over greens. Remove heavy stems.
Wash 3 or 4 more times until last water is clear and free
of grit or sand. Chop greens and set aside. Bring water,
salt, pepper, and fatback to a boil in a big heavy pot. Add
washed turnip greens, stirring them down as they wilt.
Cover and simmer briskly 1 hour.

Yield: 4 servings
1 cup chicken stock may be added. (optional)

Chapter 9

Connie rose early the next morning. She reached over to click on the radio on the nightstand next to the bed. She brought two radios with her. The alarm clock radio on the nightstand she had ever since college, and the larger table model radio she bought for her kitchen counter after she and Anthony got married. Connie fiddled around to find a radio station that played gospel music; *black gospel music.* No matter where she turned the dial, nothing seemed to satisfy what she was looking for.

Not wanting to waste any more time she headed down the hallway towards the bathroom to wash up at the sink. Just at the opening of the living room, a thought sprang into her head–the stereo. Yes! That was it. She would put on one of the gospel albums her folks used to play on Sunday mornings. Connie surveyed the albums and selected the recording by Mahalia Jackson. "Now", she said out loud, "That's the Contralto voice that makes it feel like Sunday morning"!

On her return trip through the hallway, she flipped the album over to the other side. Hearing the songs from the bedroom bought back meaningful memories.

Connie smiled when she realized she had picked up some of her Mother's habits. She put on all of her undergarments, and what little makeup she was going to wear. She left the sponge rollers in her hair, and put her house robe back on. Then she took a scarf from the top dresser drawer and wrapped it around her head. If she was just going to have a bowl of cold cereal, and a slice of toast she would not have gone through that ritual.

But, she had decided to have bacon and eggs for breakfast. She knew this was something she picked up from Minnie Mae Webster. This wasn't the first time she had performed these extra steps. She had done it many times before; but standing in her Mother's bedroom, and catching a glimpse of herself in the mirror, solidified the fact that she was indeed her Mother's daughter.

When Connie had gotten a little older she asked her mother why she put her robe back on when she cooked. Her Mom told her it was to keep the cooking odors out of her hair, and to keep food odors from seeping into her clothing. She said there was nothing worse than sitting next to someone who smelled like rancid lard, or bacon grease.

It also kept her from sending her good dresses and suits back and forth to the cleaners so often. She told Connie the chemicals they used were harsh they would cause the fabric to weaken and wear your clothes thin before their time.

Connie cleaned up the kitchen, and finished dressing for church. She went to the floor length mirror and checked both the front of her appearance, and the back. She grabbed her Bible and her purse from the Queen Ann chair, and headed for the front door. Reflecting on the last ritual performed, she shook her head back and forth. Then, reaching for the door knob she said, "You are Your Mother's child!"

Connie had to admit she was a little nervous about attending church this morning. St. James Church was less than a mile straight up the road. She remembered walking that distance twice a week before her father got a used vehicle. *It's kind of funny*, she thought, *when you say today that something is a mile or two down the road, it seems like you're talking about something that is a long way off. But, back then, when I was a child, it was only a hop, skip, and a jump away.*

Connie leaned towards the center of the car to check her face in the rearview mirror. She wanted to be sure she hadn't put her lipstick on to heavily. She wasn't one to pile on the makeup anyway, but sometimes what's applied in a bedroom mirror can look a whole lot different in the light of day.

Connie put her Chevy Impala in reverse, and backed it out of the driveway. She had only gone two doors down past sister Miller's house, and saw a car in the unpaved driveway. Connie thought the old Buick may have belonged to the visiting grandson, but she wasn't sure. It could have belonged to one of Mrs. Miller's grown children whose still lived with her; or to one of them who may have come back home to stay with her. Either way it seemed that Mrs. Miller had a ride to church.

She used to be one of the neighbors that her parents picked up on Sunday mornings. Others who lived further up the road would walk, but when the weather was inclement, Pop would offer them a ride to church too. Sometimes when we arrived at church, as many as nine to ten people would pour out of the car. That included a baby who was held by its Mama, and a couple of smaller children who had to sit on our laps.

Before she realized it, Connie saw the sign for St. James CME church. The marquee publicized the sermon for the day: "Your Christianity – Is It Real, or Is It Memorex?" Wow! Connie thought, *I can't imagine old pastor Dixon preaching something new and upbeat as that.* Her eyes moved down to the bottom of the board. It read: James Thornton, Pastor. "What? *What happened to Pastor Dixon? Olivia never said anything to me about a new pastor.*
Come to think of it, neither did Edmund.

There must've been about twenty-five, or thirty cars on the premises. And what do you know, they were all parked on a paved parking lot. Connie was baffled. *What's going on here* she thought? *Am I at the right St. James Church*? It dawned on her that she never asked Levee if the church was still up the street. *Nah! That would've been something Levee would have told me from the beginning.* She had to be in the right place.

Connie had been home often enough to remember if the church had moved or not. *For Pete's sake!* She thought, *it's only been fourteen months since Mama's Home Going celebration. Was the new Pastor here then? Because Pastor Dixon did the service, I probably didn't notice someone else was pastoring the church then.*

Cars were parked on both sides of the building. The

church faced the street, and on her way through the parking lot, Connie noticed a few signs mounted on polls that indicated certain parking spaces closer to the church. On her way in the building her eyes fell on one of the reserved spaces. It was for **Pastor Dixon.**

Connie entered the vestibule, and noticed some other changes had taken place too. There were friendly faces to greet her once she got inside the door. These people seemed to be genuinely happy to see her. The person greeting her reached out to shake her hand and said "Welcome to St. James, My name is–she gave her name, as did the greeter standing across from her at the other door. She asked for my name and wanted to know if I was visiting, or if I was someone's special guest for today. I told her yes, and no, that I just moved back into town and St. James was the church I grew up in.

Just as I started to give her Levee's name, I looked up and saw her coming in my direction. She was waving one hand in the air, and half-way dragging Earl Junior (her four year old) alongside of her. She was nearly out of breath when she reached me. Levee let the greeter know that I was her sister.

I leaned down to say hello to my nephew, and gave him a big kiss on the cheek. I was in the midst of telling him how much I missed him when he reached his hand up and wiped the side of his face. He wiped the spot where I had planted the kiss. Seeing that, I thought I had left a lipstick smudge on his face. I opened my purse and took out a handkerchief to wipe it off. Olivia started to laugh. I looked at her, and asked what was so funny. She shook her head from side to side, and began to explain.

"I should have warned you. He wipes his face off after anyone kisses him, even me. He just started doing that about two months ago. I guess that comes along with being four years old." "I'm sorry, I didn't know." "Oh, that's all right. I guess it'll be something new when he turns five."

Olivia gave her stomach sort of a *pat-rub*.

"At least it's given me some practice for the next one that's coming along."

"By the way, when are you due?" "Well, the doctors say I'm due the first week in December. I'm a little past the second week in my fifth month, but I feel like I'm as big as a house." Connie assured Olivia that she looked just fine. As they walked around the corner to go in the side doors of the sanctuary, Connie asked Levee about some of the changes that had taken place around the church.

She noticed a lot of new things about the church. The church had grown up in more ways than one. There must have been 100 members added to the congregation since she belonged there nearly nine years ago. Olivia said since summer vacation had not ended, and school wouldn't begin until after Labor Day, some families were still on vacation. She said there were still maybe another 20 to 25 people who were not in church today. Levee said she could tell by the number of children who were not in Sunday school classes. Many of the classrooms were missing students.

Connie was happy to see that Pastor Dixon was still very much involved in the flow of happenings at St. James church. The choir was great, and the sermon was dynamic! Not only was Pastor Thornton a product of

Bible college and Seminary, but he was Spirit-filled, and *Fire-Baptized*! Connie was so stirred by the music, and moved by the preaching, it must have been near the end of the sermon before she recognized the other man sitting on the platform next to Pastor Dixon. She thought to herself, *'I know I glanced that way a few times before when Pastor Dixon, and the other brothers were encouraging the preacher with their support of Amen, but those glances were quick'.*

This time Connie looked towards the pulpit because she thought she felt someone's eyes looking at her. When her eyes caught the gentleman's glance, he quickly turned his head toward the preacher. But, there was no mistake about it. It was Otis–*Otis Delaney*, her high school, and college sweetheart. He was older. He had a thin mustache, and surprisingly he was sporting close cut sideburns, but it was him. *What was he doing on the pulpit in St. James Church?* At that point, he stood and briskly walked across the platform to carry a fresh handkerchief to Pastor Thornton. He removed the one Pastor Thornton previously used to wipe the sweat from his face. When the message was over Pastor Dixon stepped to the podium to offer a call to salvation for those who did not know Christ as their Lord and personal Savior.

Connie's attention was drawn back to Otis, who now poured a glass of water for Pastor Thornton. He picked up a small white hand towel from the chair beside him to wipe the perspiration from the back of Pastor's neck. He placed the small towel around the preacher's collar. Next he took the Bible and the folder the pastor preached from, and placed them in an attaché case that sat on the floor beside the small round table. The table was between the two Pastor's chairs. *What in the world!* This was all new to Connie.

Before the service ended, a young lady came to a smaller podium that was at floor level, to give the announcements, and to recognize any visitors that may have joined them for service that morning.

Chapter 10

The person who gave the announcements read off several items. My mind must've been preoccupied because I don't remember her saying why the refreshments were being served after church in the fellowship Hall. She did say she hoped their visitors would stay and join them. One of the new things at St. James were the posted signs, not just in the parking lot area, but inside the building too. When I came in to the church I noticed a sign directly in front of me over the double doors that led into the sanctuary. The sign read SANCTUARY.

On either side of the sanctuary doors (at eye level) were signs with an arrow directing you to the Church Office on the left, and the other sign that directed you to Classrooms on the right. Both wall plaques also had the word *Restroom* inscribed on them; letting you know there were restrooms to the right and left of where you were. Not only were the signs new, but so was the other bathroom. The new restroom could have already been installed when I came for Mama's Home going Service, but I'm sure I even noticed it.

A few of the older saints caught up with me before Levee and I left the sanctuary. They hugged, squeezed, and kissed me on the side of the cheek. Some welcomed me back home, and other wanted to begin their "*I remember When*" conversations, but in a gentle manner,

Levee would excuse us so we could move on to someone else.

We left out of the sanctuary by one of the side doors, and there in front of me was another plaque on the wall. It had the words: FELLOWSHIP HALL, engraved on it, and an arrow that pointed to the right. It wasn't that the church was that big (I smiled to myself) but the new changes did promote a sense of growth. I could see that the timing for Pastor Thornton and his family was just right. The young lady that did the announcements reminded the congregants of their building fund campaign, saying if they had not yet met their pledge obligations the time was drawing nigh.

Connie had so many questions to ask her sister, but they could wait until later. It was evident that Earl Jr. was anxious to get to some refreshments, and seemingly so was Olivia. But, then again if I were in her condition, I would have been too. We entered through the small double doors that now had the words Fellowship Hall over its threshold. I remembered when it used to be called the kitchen.

Olivia stepped to one side, and applauds and cheers flooded the room. I was flabbergasted! Pastor Dixon and Pastor Thornton were standing up front at the cafeteria style window opening to the kitchen. They stood under a painted banner that had the words: **Welcome Home Constance** on it. I didn't know what to do. I couldn't move.

Olivia grabbed my hand and headed through the small crowd. I waved at a familiar face or two, and then turned in the direction of those who called my name. I waved at Elaine Carter, and many of my old friends. I wasn't sure if all of them attended St. James church, or if they just came out today for the welcome home event. Pastor Dixon elevated his voice above the noise in the room to get everyone's attention.

He made a short speech while I stood by his side. Mother Dixon greeted me with tears in her eyes. I knew she was thinking of Mom and Pop. Then, Pastor Dixon introduced me to Pastor Thornton and his family. He said he was sorry he never met me before this event, but he had heard so much about me from my family that he felt he almost knew me.

My eyes couldn't help but notice the tall, handsome gentleman who stood directly to the left, but slightly behind Pastor Thornton. Otis gave me a knowingly smile, and a slight nod of his head. Pastor Thornton must have followed my eye movement, and cut off what he had been saying.

"Oh, excuse my manners. Allow me to introduce my armor bearer Mrs. Black. This is Deacon Otis Delaney."

Otis extended his hand, and it was strong, but warm and gentle. It felt like the sincerity of an old friend. Then Pastor Thornton said, "I believe you two know each other, am I right?" My eyes darted at him a little too quickly, and my face must have expressed a questioning look. He immediately explained himself by saying; "What I meant to say is, I understand you and Deacon Delaney went to high school together."

Someone called for his attention, and excusing himself from our presence, he went through the assembly to greet other parishioners and guest. Otis realized he was still holding Connie's hand from their introduction, and a wave of embarrassment came over his face. He recovered by giving her hand another hearty shake, and then released his grip. To break the awkward situation, Connie cleared her throat and said, "Did I hear Pastor Thornton call you Deacon Delaney?"

"Yes you did. Well to make a long story short, over the past few years I've suffered through so many trials and disappointments, I can truly say that serving as Deacon in the Christian church has been one of the highlights in my life, but the first was accepting Jesus as my Lord and Savior."

Connie managed to paste a weak smile on her face, because she couldn't help but feel that one of those disappointments had been her. What could have been another awkward moment for the both of them was interrupted by Olivia.

There were a few more friends of the family and other acquaintances who wanted to say hello to me. Earl and Levee had invited me to dinner at their house. I knew my sister wanted to get home to put finishing touches on the meal. I also wanted to get home to change into something more comfortable. Leaving the fellowship hall, I happened to look over my shoulder to see Edmund chatting with Otis. Catching her eye, Edmund gave her a wave, and cupped his hands on either side of his mouth in order to carry his voice over the crowd.

"I'll see you at Levee's." I didn't want to holler back across the room, so I raised my hand indicating the familiar okay sign. I saw Mrs. Miller in the parking lot. She and a few others from her household were headed towards the older model Buick LeSabre. I quickened my pace across the newly paved parking lot to catch up with them. I thanked her again for the pound cake, and then I recognized the driver of the car. It was Mrs. Miller's oldest daughter, Joyce.

Connie thought how she never really knew Joyce that well, because she had married and moved out of the house while Connie was still in junior high school. She saw Joyce every now and then when she came by to visit her mother, but because there was such an age difference between them, they were never what one would call close friends.

She was closer in age to Philip, one of Joyce's younger brothers, but he was still a few grades ahead of her in school. Connie always thought that Philip liked her, but maybe he knew her father wouldn't hear of a boy in high school trying to talk to his daughter. At the time I was only in junior high.

———

Connie hung up her Sunday clothes, and changed into something more comfortable for lounging around and eating. She called her sister's house to see if she could bring any extras to help with the meal. Other than a few more slices of pound cake Olivia said no. Connie cut more than ample servings for all, and wrapped the slices in aluminum foil. The house seemed pretty warm, and it had not even gotten to the hottest part of the day. She decided to set up her little ritual with the air-conditioner and the fans.

Just as she had those steps the telephone rang, and thinking Levee had called back because she remembered something else, Connie picked up the extension in the kitchen before it rang again. "Hello."
"Hello Constance." It was a man's voice, but there was something different about it. Connie thought this was going to be one of her brother's practical jokes, so she beat him to the punch.

"Okay sir, or whoever you may be. I have a college education, so I don't need your encyclopedias. I have plenty of Tupperware, **and** I don't need to order any of your magazines that can register me to win $10,000 from *your* clearinghouse. Is there anything else I forgot?"

"Well Ma'am, I'm not quite sure."
After hearing the gentleman's voice again, Connie had a feeling she had made a big mistake. She thought the voice was somewhat familiar. There was a pause, and then the caller spoke again.
"Is this Constance Webster, I mean Constance Black?" She eased into her next response. "Yes it is… Who is this please?"
"This is Otis—Otis Delaney."
Connie was so embarrassed. How on earth could she have embarrassed herself with that mouth of hers two times in the same day, and with the same person!

She had just spoken with him at church. Why didn't she remember his voice?

"Oh my God! I'm so sorry. Yes… yes this is she." Connie stumbled through her words. I mean to say, yes this is me. I thought you were my brother Eddie." She was so embarrassed she didn't know what to say. Thank goodness Otis spoke up first. "I'm sorry for the misunderstanding, and the confusion. I know you must be on your way out. Your brother told me that all of you had an engagement at your sister's house today."

So, Connie thought to herself, *that's how he got my number.* I know it's supposed to be registered with the telephone company soon, but this is *way* too early for it to have been publicized.

"Yes, I was just on my way out."
"Then I won't keep you. I didn't know if you heard the announcement this morning about the Labor Day picnic event."

"I think I did, but to be honest with you, I'm not sure I caught all of what was being said." Connie didn't want to say because she was preoccupied looking at him.

"Well, the men and the deacons are sponsoring the picnic, and if you aren't otherwise engaged, I'm inviting you as my special guest."

Connie wasn't exactly sure what that meant, *my special guest*, but before she could respond to the invitation, Otis cut through her pondering saying: "Hey, look, I know this is kind of short notice, and you are on your way out, so why don't I give you a call later on. I can fill you in on the details then."

"Okay. I'd appreciate that."

"All right, then I guess I'll talk with you later on. Goodbye."

"Goodbye and thank you for the call." Connie placed the receiver back on its cradle, and still in somewhat of a fog asked herself: *Now, what was that all about?*

Chapter 11

The ride to Levee's house followed the tracks down to the main intersection that parted Stone Quarry, Georgia North and South sides. By crossing over the Vie Dock onto South Central; Stone Quarry was divided East and West depending on which way you traveled. Connie traveled a few blocks up towards Central, and turned left at the light on Central and Springfield Avenue. That was the intersection that led to Levee's house on East Claymont St.

It wasn't a long drive, but even so less than twenty years ago the homes in that section of town were for *whites* only. Of course, people like my parents could come and work in this part of town. They could clean people's homes, and help raise their children–they just couldn't own any property on that side of the tracks.

Connie tried her best not to think of the phone call she received almost twenty minutes ago. One being, that she was still peeved over embarrassing herself. She consoled herself with the thought that anyone could have made the same mistake. After all, who could tell who a person is with just one simple *Hello?*

Connie wasn't sure how she was really feeling, because her feelings were all mixed up. What was Edmund thinking about? Why did he give her phone number out to someone whom she hadn't spoken to in years? Why didn't he ask her permission first? Connie applied the brakes, and steered the car into her sister's concrete driveway, and parked in back of Edmund's car.

An irritating thought panged her mind. What if it's not just family was invited to this Sunday dinner? *That is the one thing she didn't want people to do… try to fix her up with somebody.* There was so much settling in she had to do. Sure, this was family and old friends, but she hadn't lived among them for almost fourteen years. She had to give her mind and her body a chance to shut down from the life she used to live in Nashville. Every thought that came into her mind made her angrier! The next thing she knew, Olivia was tapping on the car window. Connie was startled out of her wits. Olivia's muffled voice came through the closed window.
"Why are you sitting in the car?"
Connie reached for the door handle, and rolled the window down. Levee was repeating her question. "Why are you out here sitting in the car? You know (she said sarcastically) we *do* have central air in the house. We are not that poor" "I'm sorry. I had something on my mind and I… I." Connie almost said she was detained by a phone call from a used to be friend, but caught herself.
"Girl, we have been holding the food waiting for you. Eddie's been here for a while, and my husband's hungrier than ever." "Okay, I'm coming."

Connie turned off the air, and the ignition, and rolled the window back up. She got out of the car, and locked the door. Following Levee into the house, she realized these safety habits she had acquired spilled over from her living in Nashville. Coming through the door felt like home and a brief look around, let her know the gathering was family only. She breathed a sigh of relief and relaxed.

At first Connie felt badly about only bringing the few slices of pound cake, but once she walked through the kitchen and out onto the patio, she could see that Levee and Earl had everything well under control.

After greeting the family for the second time today, she turned her attention towards Edmund. She couldn't wait to get at him. When he saw her heading his way with a certain look on my face, he knew he was in trouble. He caught the drift. He knew he should not have given Otis her telephone number without asking her first. But Edmund knew how interested Otis would get every time he shared something with him about Connie. And after hearing that she was coming back home to live here permanently, he was anxious to speak with her again.

Edmund was working up a good defense for himself just in case Otis had jumped the gun, and called Connie right away, and from the look on her face, it appeared he had. Connie gently, but forcibly led her brother from the patio into the living room. Without as much as a hesitant breath, Connie lit into her brother.

"Edmund, I could slap you! Why did you give *that* man my telephone number? My phone number is my private business, and I'll choose who I want to give it to."

Edmund drew in a deep breath in order to speak, but before he could get one word out of his mouth, Connie continued on with her rampage.

87

Now Connie had her hands waving in the air, and she was pacing back and forth.

"What in the world were you thinking? I'm a grown woman; not a little school girl who needs you to fix her up with the date. I'm trying to get my life settled again… to get it back to some kind of normalcy. I don't know what I'm going to do about my finances. I have to think about getting a job, and the last thing I need right now is to have some *old flame* thinking of times gone by trying to pick up from where he left off."

Edmund had listened to all he was about to from his sister. He moved in front of her to block her pacing. Connie lifted her head up to look in his face. Edmund was looking her dead in the eyes. A stern expression clamped his face, and through clenched teeth he said: "I've heard everything you've had to say, now it's my turn to say something."

Connie started to protest, but Edmund raised his hand in front of her face with his pointer finger sticking straight up in the air. He repeated himself in almost a hushed-tone of voice. "Now, it's my turn to talk", he said. This time his words were spaced apart; letting each one of them hang on a note of its own. Connie was awestruck. At that moment he came off sounding, and *looking* so much like Edmund Sr., that goose bumps covered her arms, and ran down her neck. Before the astonishment of her shock gave way to her emotions, she voluntarily backed herself into a chair, and plopped down.

Edmund wanted to respect Connie as his older sister, so before he spoke he toned his voice down a bit. And, because she was sitting, he took a seat too, as not to be towering over her. He first apologized for giving out her phone number without her permission, and gently reminded her that it wasn't a private number; that it was soon to be listed in the local telephone directory. Edmund also reminded her quickly, that just because she left town, the rest of the family didn't.

He said he didn't know what happened that caused the breakup between her and Otis, but the fact was that ever since Otis gave his life to the Lord, and became a member of St. James Church, they had become friends. The six years between their ages that use to make a difference in school, no longer existed between them as men. They were now comrades in the faith.

Edmund told Connie he knew he wasn't as wise as she was, but when all was said and done; whether she realized it or not, it wouldn't hurt to have at least one other person in town that she could call *friend*; and all the better if it were a male friend for times when maybe he wasn't around.

During the meal, the family laughed about old times. Connie told Olivia about finding the recipe cards; which she also never remembered Mama using. Every now and then she and Edmund's eyes would meet, and there was a certain unexpressed *knowing* that their relationship as sister and brother had now reached another level.

The evening ended around 5:00pm for everyone. The day had been long, but eventful. When Connie got home, she went to the bedroom and kicked off her shoes. Then she went to the living room to relax in front of the TV. Maybe she could catch most of the Ed Sullivan show. She reflected on the happenings of the day: the changes at church, the new pastor, the sermon, *Deacon* Otis Delaney, the surprise *Welcome Home* celebration, the phone call, and the dispute with her brother.

Connie's attention focused on the television when she heard Ed Sullivan announce the name Ella Fitzgerald. *Well, she thought, what do you know about that?* One of *us* is on the show tonight. She went to the television and turned the volume higher.

Chapter 12

Connie turned the radio on in the kitchen while she fixed some toast and cold cereal for breakfast. She knew she could get by another good month or so without additional income, but she also knew she would have start to start looking for employment in the next couple of weeks.

One of the things on her mind was to start getting the local newspaper. She would see about picking one up at the Winn Dixie this afternoon, then she would call the main newspaper office to see about getting delivery started.

The news anchor on the radio this morning was updating a story from last month. McDonald's CEO Sarah Casanova, had setbacks in the restaurants in Japan. The problem was with the tainted chicken meat coming out of the factory in China. It seems the products were being used past their use-by date. The next news item really caught her attention, because it was happening right then. Unemployment was edging up. President Nixon announced a new economic policy. A ninety-day wage-price freeze, a stimulated tax cut, and a temporary 10 percent tariff and spending cut was in effect as of this month.

Wow! *How will that affect my job search*? Connie rinsed her cereal bowl and saucer, and set them in the sink. She ran a glass of tap water and swallowed her multi-vitamin pill. The anchor now reflected on the July 31st Apollo15 astronauts who supposedly had taken a six-and-a-half-hour electric car ride on the surface of the moon. Connie couldn't help but wonder, *with all the money they spend on research in outer space, why can't some of it go to decrease the rising unemployment situation?*

Connie took a peek at her 'To Do' list lying on the table. *Humm*, she thought—*dusting*! That was something she didn't have to do often when she lived in her upstairs apartment in Nashville. The windows stayed shut most of the time, and in the summer she used the air conditioner.

On her way to the bedroom to get a scarf from the second dresser drawer Connie realized she might have double duty to do. Not only was the downstairs twice the size of her former apartment, but if the living and dining rooms needed dusting, they also needed to be vacuumed. The same dust that came in from the window having been hoisted up, not only settled on the table tops and lamps, but on the carpet and floor as well.

Connie realized she really let herself in for some chores today. She smiled to herself *at* using the word *'chores'*. Her mind went back to when she grew up in this very house. Everyone had their chores to do. She went to the pantry to get the vacuum cleaner. Connie stop for a moment and think. *Now, what comes first, the dusting or the vacuum*? Looking at the old upright, she spoke out loud, "**the vacuuming**". A new vacuum cleaner was one of the items she wanted to get for the house, but not now. She'd have to wait until income was flowing into the pot, not out of it. Because the attached bag was loose fitting, it released a little residue. Not enough to be a great problem, however it would benefit her to vacuum, and then dust afterwards. That way she would only have to dust once.

———————

Otis finished shaving, but didn't move from the sink. He was still looking in the mirror. He really wasn't looking at himself, but gazing past the image in the mirror and into what was running across his head. *Man, you jumped the gun! You moved in on Constance like a desperate criminal. You know you blew it don't you? Just because you have loved her since high school, doesn't mean she feels the same way about you. After all, you were the one running wild.*

Otis remembered how everything went pretty good her first year of college. And things were still running smoothly when she came home for the summer, but when she went back (he thought to himself) I was the one who started tipping out on her. When she came home for the Christmas holiday they were still pretty much a couple, but by the time the next summer break came around, he was the one backing off. She was even willing to get engaged, but *that* word scared him. His knucklehead friends convinced him to play the field before he settle down. What a mistake! When the news got back to Connie that he had seen a few other chicks who, let's say didn't have much of a *pure* reputation, she broke it off with him. I didn't blame her. We met and dated in high school as virgins, and we made vows to each other to remain that way until God joined us together in Holy matrimony.

Otis looked down at his watch and realized the minutes had ticked away. He quickly dressed, then headed for his small storefront shop. The shop had a large open room in the front, a small room in the back, a bathroom and a closet. Actually, the bathroom consisted of a sink and a toilet. Otis had saved a little money from when he worked on construction jobs several years back. When Belinda divorced him, he was attending DeVry School of Technology trying to earn a degree in electronics. Otis worked full-time in a local department store in downtown Atlanta as an elevator operator, and did handy man's work on the side
whenever he had the spare time. He had put most of the experience of his bad marriage behind him now. What it all boiled down to was that his wife didn't want to be married to him anymore. No matter what he did, it was not good enough for her. The more he tried to anchor his faith in the Lord, the more distant she became.

Otis turned on the air conditioner mounted in the front window, and bought out one of the repairs he was working on. He put it on the small worktable behind the counter. When he was fixing up the shop for business, he built the counter a little lower than a usual walk-up business counter would have been. He did that so when customers bought in their small television sets, and radios for repair, they wouldn't struggle in getting them on the counter.

The waist-high counter also made it easier for him to see customers when they came through the door, because sometimes he was seated at the table working. Otis did all the work himself to refurbish the rundown office space. He repaired the roof, the leaks and the plumbing. He even re-spackled and painted the walls.
He laid down the new linoleum floor, and wired the back room and bathroom for electricity.

Otis fiddled around with the old radio until he found the source of the problem. He was glad he took a business and accounting course when he attended DeVry. It came in handy for knowing how to acquire a tax number ID, and ordering his repair tubes and parts at wholesale prices. That way, he had his own supply stocked right in the back room, and he made a little extra money selling tubes and parts to others who knew how to repair their own radios and TV's. Most people didn't mind buying parts from him, because they knew he still beat the prices of the name brand supply stores. Otis would even let them look at the supply catalog to order the part they needed. He knew the catalog listed the retail price. Of course, he would order for the shop at the wholesale cost still making a little profit on the side.

While sitting there working, his mind drifted back to his failed marriage. Belinda never appreciated anything he did. It had to be all about her. If it wasn't for the fact that he'd messed up with Constance, he would have never paid any attention to her—at least he never did when they were in high school. Oh it's not that she didn't try. He just never went for her type. She was pretty enough, but she knew it too. She had the looks, so he couldn't understand why she seemed to be so jealous of all her girlfriends. She purposely flirted with the other girl's boyfriends to try and break the couple up. If she succeeded, she would date the guy for a month or two, and then drop the poor *sucker. He only used that word because he knew it applied to him now.*

Belinda liked to party, and run to the clubs. Most times she went with her girlfriends, because he had to study for a test, or either work his part-time job. He remembered being excited when he thought she was pregnant. She said she had missed a cycle or two, but after coming from the doctors, she told him it was a false alarm. She said she was one of those girls who had an irregular monthly flow. So, as much as she had hoped she was going to have a baby, it turned out to be a false alarm.

Just those couple of years into the marriage, he knew he had made a big mistake. He told himself more than once that Belinda was not tipping out on him, so he tried to ignore her actions. It wasn't until one night at Bible study that his grandmother approached him with something she thought he ought to know. He often went to her for advice and she knew his situation. She would pray with him about his concerns. His grandparents were the only parents he had, or at least that he remembered having. They raised him from the age of four years old.

That night reality kicked him in the seat of his pants. Sure enough when he drove around to the Motor Lodge, his wife was laid up in the bed with another man. Otis chuckled to himself, not because anything was funny, but because he was thankful how well God knew him. He could laugh about it now because he didn't own a weapon back then. *All I had when I broke into their motel room was my car keys, and Jesus. Thank God for Jesus!*

The next day he told Belinda to leave his house, and take all of her things with her. Then she did one of the meanest, vindictive things that any woman could do to any man. She knew how hurt he was in finding her with another man, but that wasn't good enough for her. She had to crush him even more. She had to pour vinegar into an open womb. Leaving out the front door, she turned with her suitcases in her hand and looked Otis in the eyes. An ugly, *devious* smirk came over her face, and she said: "0h, by the way, I was pregnant and lease twice during this stupid marriage. That's right! I had two abortions, and I'm not sure if any of those babies were yours, but now we'll never know… will we?"

Otis slammed the door so hard it almost came off its hinges. He made his way into the bathroom, and vomited until his insides were raw.

Chapter 13

The ding-a-ling of the bell attached to the top of the door molding bought Otis out of his musing. A small voice interrupted him. "Are you all right Mr. Delaney?"

It was Mrs. Cunningham, one of his elderly customers. Otis realized he had tears on his cheeks, and his nose had begun to run. He quickly half stood up, and grabbed a handkerchief from his hip pocket. He moved toward the counter wiping his eyes, and taking care of his nose.

"Oh no, Mrs. Cunningham, I'm okay. It's just that, I mean I had a little…" Otis really didn't know what he was trying to say. "That's alright young man. I understand. I used to suffer with Hay Fever myself. Of course that was years ago. I was much younger then, but I've outgrown it now. Oh mercy me, I don't know why I said I've outgrown it now (ha ha), I was grown when I got it."

Otis was trying to get a word in edgewise to tell Mrs. Cunningham that he didn't have Hay Fever, but thought, '*what's the use.*' He found an opening before she could get her second wind. It wasn't any use telling her he didn't have Hay Fever. By now she probably was on her way to giving him a good cure. He moved from behind the counter to the back room to get the old radio from the shelf where he kept the items that had been repaired. When he got back Mrs. Cunningham was still talking, mainly to herself, about what she used to do when she had Hay Fever.

"I bet you came by to pick up your radio, and here it is." He placed the radio on the countertop. He unwrapped the cord so he could plug it into the outlets he had rigged-up on one of the polls under the counter. He always liked for his customers to see that their television, or radio was working fine before they left his shop.

"One of the tubes blew out. It was one of the larger ones I didn't have in stock, so I had to order it out of the catalog (he was quick to add), but it won't cost you one penny more. You only pay the price quoted to you. I pay whatever the company charged me for shipping."

Mrs. Cunningham paid the $10.00 charge, but not without complaining about the high cost of everything now-a-days. She said, "They (*speaking of manufactures*) just don't make things like they used to. These tubes blow out like twinkle lights."

Otis agreed with her, even though he knew that her radio was more than twenty years old, and ever since the transistor radio hit the market, it was getting harder to find the tubes to repair old radios like hers.

Connie sat at the kitchen table reading through the WANT ADS. She was glad she left the air-conditioner on and the fans running when she left the house. The house was comfortable, but not cold. She had never been one for the ice cold temperatures of air-conditioning in the house. Maybe it was because they did without it for so long when she was growing up. It was convenient, but costly. With that thought running across her mind, Connie went to the bedroom and turned the unit off. The fans were still circulating the cool air throughout the house. Knowing that would last for a while, Connie poured a glass of lemonade from the pitcher in the refrigerator, and went back to reading her paper.

It was evident her mind had lost the intensity of searching for employment. She was randomly thumbing through the pages, not resting her eyes on anything in particular. What her mind *did* rest on were the events of yesterday; especially the phone call from Otis.

Connie folded the paper, and leaned back in her chair. Otis said he would call me later. Suppose he called when I was out? She found herself wondering if she should get one of those answering machines that people hook up to their telephones. 'Nah', she thought out loud. "That's silly! When am I worrying about missing phone calls?" She got up from her seat, took her glass of lemonade, and headed for the Parlor.

Connie had an urge to look through her high school yearbook. She got a kick out of how old-timey and mature all the kids looked in the photos, even though they were all teenagers. It could have been because all of the pictures were taken in black and white. The only thing in color was the front and back cover, the insert pages that separated the grade levels, and one or two of the school activities.

But if she was to be honest with herself, she really wanted to turn to the picture of Otis Delaney. She didn't have to look up his name in the index to find the page numbers his picture was on. She knew exactly which pages to turn to. Connie looked at the photo and tried to focus on the good times, and the fun they had together when they were dating. Even so, she felt a sudden pang of grief. She knew she was well over those feelings for Otis by now, maybe something was surfacing because of the recent grief in her life. When people leave out of your life it still stirs up the grief from the past all over again.

She found the page where the two of them were pictured together. Not just the two of them, but the entire Glee Club. She was a fair singer and even sang in the choir at church before she went off to college. But Otis was a *really* good singer. She remembered some of the popular songs that were out when they were in high school. Songs like: "You're So Fine", and "Oh What A Night". The song that Otis used to sing to her that gave her goosebumps was "Earth Angel" by the Penguins. She remembered how his mellow voice would make her feel all warm and mushy inside.

Connie thought back to when Otis and a few of his friends thought they would get together a singing group. They were pretty good too. They even sang at a couple of Friday night dances at school. That was one of the few outings her folks allowed her to go to. It was chaperoned by some of the teachers, along with a couple of parents. However, with graduating from high school, getting summer jobs, and preparing to leave for college; life began to happen and they found themselves scattered; along with their hopes of becoming famous.

Connie took a sip of her now watered-down lemonade. She wondered if Otis still had that *sensual* kind of voice that made a girl swoon.

It was well past three o'clock in the afternoon and the direct sun light beaming through the Parlor windows had heated the room immensely. Connie closed the yearbook, and put it back on the shelf. She picked up her glass and wiped the water ring from the stand. It already felt cooler in the Foyer then it did sitting in the Parlor. She stood in the hallway between the living room and the dining room trying to decipher what she should do next. She wasn't used to having this much time on her hands, but she knew she wasn't quite ready to probe through the newspaper again to look for a job.

Connie still wasn't ready to lay aside her daydreaming. She decided to wash a small load of white clothes. While the wash machine was running, she could sit out on the back stoop in the old wicker rocker.

She gathered together a few soiled bath towels and facecloths, and then grabbed the linen tablecloth and napkins from the large dining room table. No use washing half a load of clothes when it takes to same amount of water to do a full load. She threw in the doilies from the sofa and armchairs in the living room. Knowing some work was getting done even while she would be relaxing she filled her drink glass again and headed for the back porch. She had to go through the door next to the stairs that led out into the garage.

Connie walked with her head up in the air, as if to tell the needed work in the garage she was ignoring it, and reached for the knob on the door that led outside.

The shade from the trees seemed to make a difference in the temperature. It was still warm out, but at least the sun was not blazing down on her. Connie sat looking out over the yard. She was thankful Edmund had cut the grass. She took in a few deep breaths and began to relax. Aside from the Oak and Pecan tree, a Silver Locus tree was also in the backyard. She knew the leaves on that particular tree would be the first to change colors for the coming autumn weather.

Her mind went back to Otis. This time she thought about the reason she broke up with him. Connie didn't feel badly about it, because even when she was that young, she never had the opinion that someone could steal your boyfriend, or girlfriend away from you. Either they wanted to be with you as your *steady*, or they didn't. She never agreed with the idea of trying to make someone stay with you when they no longer wanted to be faithful to that relationship. After all, people had a free-will.

Connie thought it was strange that thoughts like those surfaced in her teen age days, and they continued until today. Of course, life had taught her a few relationship lessons over the years, but that's all a part of growing up. Everyone has to make their own mistakes... the question is if you will learn from them.

A familiar sound of nature and the rustling of leaves near the top of the Oak tree brought Connie out of her musing. She looked up to see a bird flying from one tree limb to another. Then, her mind went to the promise of a certain phone call, and she felt the slight fluttering of butterflies, not in the air, but in her stomach. The feeling caught her off guard, and an inquisitive questioning came into her spirit.

Old Fashion Pound Cake

1 pound butter (2 cups)
1 pound sifted cake flour (4 cups)
10 large eggs, separated
1 pound sugar **(2 cups)** can be sifted–optional
1 teaspoon vanilla extract

Refrigerated items are best used at room temperature. Pre heat oven 325°F

Cream butter, work in flour until mixture is mealy. Beat egg yolks, sugar and vanilla until thick and fluffy. Add first mixture of butter and flour gradually into second mixture, beating thoroughly. Fold in stiffly beaten egg whites. Beat mixture vigorously for 5 minutes. Bake in floured tube pound cake pan, or 2 loaf pans (8x4 in.) Bake for 1¼ hours.
Testing for doneness: An inserted wooden toothpick should come out dry with no moisture on it.

Chapter 14

The regular operating hours for OD's Supply and Repair Shop were from 9:00 am to 5:00 pm Monday through Friday. On Saturdays the shop was opened from 9:00 am to 12:00 pm for those customers who couldn't get there during the week. Sometimes Otis would stay over a little later on the weekdays if a customer called ahead of time saying they were on their way if he could stay open a few minutes longer. They would have to be there within the next 10 to 15 minutes. Otis didn't mind because all he had to do was go home and watch TV.

Today he wanted to close the shop right on time because he had a delivery to make on his way home. Mondays were not his money making days. People usually dropped their radios and televisions off at the beginning of the week. His busiest pickup days were Thursdays through Saturdays. Other than Mrs. Cunningham, all the business he had today was one man who dropped off a TV that needed an antenna, and a sale for a spindle. The customer needed the one that fit over the regular spindle on his stereo so he could play his 45rpm records.

The telephone call he promised to make to Constance was on his mind all day. He didn't know if he should call her while he was still at work, or if he should wait until he got back home. Otis thought about how he jumped the gun on yesterday, and decided that he would wait until he got home.

Connie sat and watched a squirrel scurrying around the yard. It climbed the tree, and ventured out onto a limb. She thought, *be careful little squirrel I've been out on that limb before.* The squirrel looked around several times, then turned back and trotted into the thickness of the branches. He finally worked his way down the trunk of the tree and darted across the yard and under a bush. Connie looked down at her watch. She thought the wash cycle should be done by now. That was enough sitting for her. She hopped up, and went to check on the laundry.

She put the wet clothes in the laundry basket, and instead of putting the clothes in the dryer she got some clothespins from the pantry. She put them in the basket on top of the clothes. Connie decided to hang the laundry on the clothesline. She felt a certain excitement about letting the clothes dry the old fashion way. She could have used the dryer, but after it was plugged up, it made a clicking noise. She figured some gear, or screw must have shifted during the move, and she wasn't quite ready to get into any household repair bills this soon.

The air was breezy and warm, just right for drying clothes. She didn't know why, but at that moment she felt a sudden closeness to her mother. Connie pinned the last doily, and brought the basket back into the house. She decided to leave the unused clothespins in the laundry basket. That way, she wouldn't have to put them back and forth every time she did laundry. Noticing that the kitchen clock had quarter after five, her mind turned towards fixing something for supper.

She knew it would be a little something added to the fixings she bought home from Olivia's house from yesterday. Connie opened the door to the refrigerator and took out a piece of barbecue chicken, the macaroni salad, and a saucer full of celery and carrot sticks that had rosette cut radishes mixed with them.

Olivia was the cook in the family. She took after their mom and grandmother. Connie thought to herself, *I do okay, but cooking isn't my passion.* Levee was so creative. Two of the dishes she made yesterday completely disappeared. One of the dishes was what she called *Fruit En Crème.* It was nothing more than grapes and pineapple tidbits. But, if I were the one serving them, they would have been in two separate bowls sitting on the table. But Levee combined the seedless green grapes with the cut up pineapple in a medium-size bowl. She blended in 1 cup of berries, sour cream, and about one fourth of a cup of packed brown sugar. Then she mixed it all up, and put it in the refrigerator to chill.

When we got to the outing, she took the bowl out of the refrigerator and sprinkled about 1 tablespoon of brown sugar over the mixture. We ate some of the fruit while we were waiting for the meat to finish grilling. We ate some more while we were eating our meal, and after dinner we ran to get what was left in the bowl. One would think that we never had eaten any fruit before! Of course, we had. We just hadn't eaten it Levee's way.

The telephone rang just as Connie was about to put the chicken in the microwave.

"Hello." "Hi Connie. Wha-cha doing?" It was Levee. Connie shared the day's events, including her "to do" list, bringing her sister up to date down to the present phone call, and putting the chicken in the microwave. However, leaving out the part about them browsing through the yearbook thinking of Otis.

"Good. That's why I'm calling. You need to get out and have a little fun. That's why I'm inviting you to the church picnic on Saturday…Now don't say no.

I know you have things to do around the house, but you need a social life too. I've got everything planned. Earl and I will pick you up around ten O' clock. The picnic starts at eleven, but we have to be there a little ahead of time to set things up. You will make your famous, delicious potato salad, and help me judge the 'Egg Walk' race."

Connie heard Olivia taking a deep breath, and didn't have time to object to anything before she said: "*Soo, how does that sound?*"

She hesitated, but went on to say that the plan sounded just fine to her. Olivia told her she didn't have to hang with her all day long, just until after they set up for the egg race. She needed someone to follow the kids up and down on the field to make sure one of the *little dears* tried putting their thumb on the egg in order to hold it on the spoon.

Actually Connie was sort of relieved, because that let her off the hook with Otis' invitation. She'd been widowed for about four and a half years now. Sure there were spurts of loneliness that crept up on her, but to be honest, she just wasn't ready to put her heart on the line again.

During the past four (almost five) years she often thought what it would have been like if she had not been so hasty in cutting Otis off. Connie knew that both of them were young at the time, and both of them had made their own mistakes. She also could tell that Otis was a changed, mature Christian man. Still, she wanted to get settled in to the idea of living back home again. Things were going to be different, to say the least—even challenging.

Trying to figure out all that comes along with being the sole owner of the family property, she didn't need the problems of being involved in a new relationship. Connie jumped when the ring of the telephone blared through the air. She had not moved from where she was when she hung up from talking to Olivia. She just knew that Levee had forgotten something else she wanted her to do. She reached for the receiver.

Chapter 15

"Yeah, what did you forget?" "Hello, Connie." It wasn't Olivia. It was Otis Delaney. Connie couldn't believe it! *How many times in two days can someone stick their foot in their mouth?"*

"Well, I can't say that I forgot anything. As a matter of fact, I'm trying to be a good steward and keep my promise to call you back." "Oh, my God! I'm so sorry. I thought you were someone else."

"Yeah, I get that all the time (Otis let out a little chuckle) but, I figured you meant that question for someone else. But I must say, I would really like to call you one of these times, and you answer the phone *not* thinking it was someone else." Connie was so embarrassed, and also at a loss for words.

"I'll tell you what. I'm going to hang up the phone, and call you right back."

Before Connie could say anything, she heard a click on the line, and after that she heard the hum of 'dial tone'. About three seconds later the telephone rang. She couldn't help but laugh. Of course, she knew it was Otis. But now, she felt a little guilty because she knew why he was calling, and she would have to turn him down. She picked up the receiver and made her voice sounds sophisticated and high-toned.

"The Constance Weber-Black Agency. How may I direct your call?" Connie heard a loud manly laugh exuding from the receiver, and she had to laugh along with him. "Now, that's how to answer a telephone." Otis decided to flirt a little. "And if this is the receptionist, I'm almost afraid to ask for the boss."

The sound of his voice and his choice of words made Connie want to flirt back, but she didn't because fear set in. "Hey there Otis, I mean *Deacon* Delaney. Thanks for calling me back." Connie's choice of words (Deacon Delaney) put a damper on things for Otis right away. But he had called to invite her to the Labor Day picnic, and it would seem silly now if he didn't follow through. He picked up on her coldness, and decided not to push the issue.

"Well Sister Black, I'll get right to the point. I extended an invitation to you about coming to the church picnic this Saturday. Have you thought about it?" "Yes. Thank you for the personal invitation. I will be coming, but I'm going with my family. My sister and brother-in-law are picking me up. We're coming over earlier so I can help Levee set up for the 'Egg Race'."
"Oh? Oh…that's great. You know what, the deacons will be there between 8:30 or 9:00 am, we have to set up the picnic tables, and get all the grills started, so I guess I'll see you on Saturday."
"Okay, and thanks again. Goodbye."
"Goodbye."
Otis tried not to let the disappointment in his voice come through the phone. Connie barely heard his goodbye. It came out in such a whisper. She could sense he was disappointed. Connie felt bad about it, but what else could she do? She didn't want an old flame to think he could just

waltz right back into her life, and pick up from where he left off fifteen years ago.

She wasn't that desperate, or was she? And if that was the case, why did she feel so awful?

Over the next couple of days Connie found herself thinking about Otis' phone call. She replayed the little hanging-up and dialed back scenario over and over again. And, each time she did, it would make her smile. It felt good to have a gentleman call her name, and to laugh with her. So, what in the heck was wrong with her? It had to be her because they're *surely* wasn't anything wrong with Otis.

———

Before Connie knew it, the end of the week rolled around. She talked with Levee a few times. She was so excited about having her sister home again. Now the whole family is together, she said. Connie could appreciate that more than ever. She felt happy about being involved; being needed. She spent the afternoon trying to figure out what outfit to wear to the picnic. She changed her mind several times before she decided on her lime green and pink Peddle-Pusher set.

It's a good thing she didn't have to dig through boxes of shoes to find her strappy sandals. Luckily her ensemble was still pretty much new. It had only been worn once, or twice. Friday evening was spent making her potato salad. Connie knew she wasn't a great cook, but Olivia was right about one thing, no one could touch her potato salad!

117

After everything was prepared and put in the fridge, Connie decided to shower and relax before going to bed. It was only nine in the evening but the temperature was still in the mid-80s. She had a marvelous idea. Instead of putting on her PJs, she put on a pair of jogging pants and a T-shirt. Connie slid the bedroom drapes to one side and opened the sliding glass door. She closed the door behind her and walked the few steps around to the front porch to sit in the swing–something she never would have done in Nashville. *Umm*, she thought, this feels nice.

The dusk of the evening had set in, but it was still light enough to see across to street and down the road. She folded her arms in back of her head, and nestled her back against the swing to give it a slight push. She swung for a while not thinking of nothing in particular. The dinging of the railroad crossing bell sounded, and she looked behind her down the road to see the flashing red lights. The cross-bar gates came down, and she heard the, woo–woo of the train whistle coming from further down the tracks. Less than a minute later, the two diesel-engines powering the locomotive came rumbling by, pulling over thirty box-cars behind them.

Connie sat there and counted each boxcar the way she and her siblings used to do when they were kids. She also remembered the warnings from their parents not to go any further than the middle of the yard when the trains were rolling down the tracks. The warning made sense to her more as an adult then it did to her as a child. She now recalled how the three of them would play a little sneaky competitive rivalry game with each other.

They would try to see which one of them could take one step farther out than the other one, just to say that they were the closest one to the train. Before they knew it they had inched their way down past the middle of the yard trying to outdo each other. It's a good thing their parents were always keeping an eye on them (knowing that children would be children). It didn't take long before they heard Mama, or Papa call out to them, and they all ended up having to sit on the front steps, or either to play in the backyard until they learned how to be obedient.

It's funny what kind of childhood memories can resurface in your thoughts. The twilight had turned into night, and the streetlights had come on. Connie went back around to the side porch to the bedroom, and closed the sliding door behind her. She clicked the lock down, and drew the drapes back in place.

Connie was up and dressed by 9:00 am. When the telephone rang, she knew it was Levee. It seems she and Earl were running a little behind because Earl Junior woke up itching. When they checked his stomach and arms, they noticed he had developed a small rash. She said she hoped it wasn't Poison Ivy. Levee sounded a little perturbed saying; "Of all the days for this to happen, why today?" She said she couldn't imagine where he'd been to get Poison Ivy. Levee said she hadn't seen Poison Ivy since our childhood days, but she was pretty sure that rash looked familiar.

119

Her husband had to wait until the drugstore opened, and he was going to take Earl with him so the pharmacist could look at the rash. That way, he would know if he needed to buy Calamine lotion, or something else. I told her not to worry I'd get Edmund to pick me up. But, she said he wasn't coming until about noon, because he had something to do downtown having to do with the Labor Day parade. We hung up settling on the fact that we would set up the booth whenever we got there, as long as it was before race which was scheduled for 12:30pm.

I questioned myself—Labor Day parade? I had forgotten all about that. I guess it's because when I grew up here years ago, *'we'* weren't in any of the Labor Day parade activities. That was just for *White* folk. You know; the people who were in those unions like the AFL – CIO, and the IBEW. Back then, they had organizations like the Lions Club, the Knights of Columbus, and the Stone Quarry Ladies' Club marching in the parades. So you know none of *us* were in it. Especially when one of the groups in the parade was waving a giant Confederate flag!

We used to stand on the sidelines watching the parade, and I remember the Mayor and Mrs. Styles waving from the motorcade. But, what got me about the float, the Labor Day Queen rode on, she was always so beautiful, and of course wearing a gown, and she was always "*white*", but that's not what bothered me the most.

Every little girl dreamed of one day being a queen, or a princess; even *'Black'* little girls. I just used to wondered how the gown and a crown were connected to *Labor*. Maybe it was because the lady had rested from her labor. I don't know. To me it seemed like they should have had a woman up there who looked like she actually worked, someone posing as 'Rosie the Riveter', or a switchboard operator.

Thank goodness the report came back negative. Earl Jr. didn't have Poison Ivy. His rash was due to strawberries. He was allergic to strawberries! It wasn't a good thing, but at least they knew he wasn't contagious. This was the first time I had ever heard of anyone in our family having an allergy. I thought I would have had a few minutes to go downtown to see the rest of the parade. If it started around 9:00 am, it still should have been going on. But, since Olivia didn't have to get a babysitter for Earl, they were going to pick me up once they had settled Earl Jr.'s itch.

Thank goodness there wasn't much to do to set up for an Egg Race. However, we did have to be *very* careful with the fresh eggs. My hope was that we had a whole lot of winners when the race was over, and not all whole lot of mess to clean up.

Chapter 16

By 11:00am the grounds began to fill up. The church was purchasing the one acre lot on the right side of the building. Even though it wasn't fully paid for, they had permission to use it. The part of the lot closest to the church didn't need clearing, or either it had already been cleared.
I'm not sure. But, that is where the activities were being held.

The picnic tables were set up on the back side of the church where the barbecue grills were. People were still coming in way after 11:00 am hauling food and drinks. Some of the crowd must have been friends and neighbors, because I'm pretty sure the congregation wasn't quite that large. Come to find out, I was right. Olivia said when they first started having this as a church Sunday school picnic it was primarily for the members. But, since then it grew into an expected outing for the neighbors, and for most of the folks on this side of the tracks as well.

Some people brought in their own picnic baskets, but they didn't have to. The church took care of everything. There were pony rides for the kids, and the Deacons funded the hiring of the two larger horses for the adults to ride—at lease for those who were brave enough to get on one. There was homemade ice cream, corn on the cob, a cotton candy machine, a jump rope contest (which was a sure sign of how old we were getting), and candy apples. Yum!

I stuck close to Levee for most of the morning. I saw Otis moving about the grounds. I wanted to say something to him, but I was afraid I'd put my foot in my mouth again. So, I did the safe thing, and helped to keep an eye on my nephew.

After our activity was over, I was freed up to do whatever I wanted. Most activities stopped around one o'clock, and everyone headed for the picnic tables to eat lunch. Earl had reserved spaces for all of us at one of the longer tables. I saw Edmund a few times. He and another guy were supervising some of the activities, and hanging on the outskirts of the property to see that the younger children didn't stray away from their parents, or run into the street. Maybe they were also keeping an eye on some of the teenagers who wanted to sneak away from parents.

I grabbed a paper plate and headed for some of the food spots. I wasn't trying to be entirely anti-social concerning Otis, because we waved to each other a few times from across the field. He didn't seem to be holding a grudge. I was sort of hoping he would want to sit with us at our table, but I didn't know if my *directness* in the phone conversation we had at the beginning of the week had put him off altogether. I was going from station to station filling my plate and saw Edmund coming over with whomever it was that he was working with.

"Hey Sis, do you remember this guy?" I turned to look at the man standing with him. He looked kind of familiar, yet my mind couldn't quite place him. I couldn't come up with a name.

"Hey Connie, you're looking good!"

The man's eyes trailed me from the top of my head and stopped at the bottom of my strappy sandals. It was a quick move, but to me it seemed like minutes. Then, his eyes locked on mine. Those eyes; yes… I remember those eyes. They were hazel brown, and dreamy. They were suggestive, and they were trouble! They belonged to none other than Marcus! How could I forget Marcus Yancey?
But, before I could say his name, he spoke up.

"It's me, Marcus. Marcus Yancey. How could you forget the guy who sat in back of you throughout high school?"
Connie remembered all right. Of course, he didn't sit in back of her in every class just Homeroom, English, History, Science and Math. *Well* she thought, *I guess it was all of my classes except for the electives.* She was dumbfounded. He was a *hunk* back then, but he was even more attractive now.
"Wow! Marcus it's good to see you again."
"And trust me, he said, May I say it's good to *see* you too?"
His eyes took another quick gander at me, and I felt that maybe I shouldn't have worn this close fitting peddle-pusher outfit. Edmund stood there like a lump on the log, not saying a word. I shot him a glance, widening my eyes. Leave it to Edmund. He got the wrong message.

This handsome man was making me feel very uncomfortable. I guess sometimes men really don't pay attention to what their buddies are insinuating to a pretty woman; especially if it's something he would be saying to a pretty girl himself. It must have just seemed natural to him.

It wasn't *what* he said. It was the way he said it with his eyes. To me, his come-on was evident, and it made me *feel* uncomfortable.

Instead of coming to my rescue, Edmund turned around and left. He said he had to get a plate and put something on it. I was mulling over in my mind if to stop Edmund or not, but by then Marcus was speaking again. "Well Constance, if I was to say you haven't changed much

I would be lying. His eyes locked on my shapely figure. You have changed. You look great!"

Connie was glad the sun was shining, and the temperature was over 90°, otherwise she would not have been able to explain the blush that flowed over her face. She waved her hand back and forth in front of her face fanning herself, and said, "My, isn't it hot out here today!"

Connie could tell Marcus wanted to keep the conversation going, but she was ready to finish putting food on her plate. Besides, out of the corner of her eye she saw Otis looking their way. He was standing near the back door entrance of the church. Marcus said he would see me in a few minutes, and went to the beginning of the line to get a plate and some plastic utensils. I finished my plate off with some barbecue ribs, and a slice of pound cake. I was pretty sure it was one of Mrs. Miller pound cakes.

Earl waved at me to get my attention. He wanted me to see the reserved table where we were sitting. I placed my plate on the table and swung my leg over the bench to have a seat. There were still a couple of spaces left at the table for others to be seated. I knew Edmund would take one of those places when he finished filling his plate, and I hoped the other person would be filled by Otis.

I still felt badly about turning him down to escort me to the picnic. I really wanted to apologize again, but what could I say: *that I was chicken*? Connie saw that Otis had moved from where he was standing. She began to scan the food area to see if he was filling his plate. Good. He was in line.

She didn't mean for him to see her looking his way, but, before she could turn back around, his eyes caught hers. Connie tried to turn her head away from his glance, but it was too late, her heart was already beating faster.

'I don't know what that was all about, not unless the brief encounter with Marcus's stirred up old memories.' I was getting ready to reach for a cup of something cool to sip on, when I realized I forgot to get my drink. Right on cue, a male voice from behind me said, "I see you didn't get anything to drink, here's a cup of lemonade"

Everything would have played out just fine if the voice behind me belonged to Otis. But, it didn't. It was Marcus. He reached over my shoulder (a little too closely if you ask me) and set the cup beside my plate. I was furious, but retained manners enough to say, *thank you.* Edmund arrived with his plate just in time to offer *Marcus* that empty space next to me. *Hum! Brothers*! I felt like going over to where the baseball game was to be held, and coming back with a bat to beat him over the head. I think the only one at the table who picked up on my feelings was Levee.

I tried to keep the attention Marcus was giving me on a positive upswing, but I was feeling so badly about what happened to Otis. He had finished filling his plate and was headed toward the table when he saw Marcus had taken the vacant space beside me. I was fuming! I hope Otis didn't think that I invited Marcus to sit with us. But, being the gentleman he was he didn't intrude. He moseyed over to the table behind ours, and sat with Pastor Thornton and his family.

Chicken and Dumplings

5-7 lb. cut up chicken	3 tsp. salt
4 cups chicken stock	2 Tbs. chopped parsley
2 onions, chopped	1 cup water
3 stalks of chopped celery	½ tsp. black pepper

Rolled Dumpling Recipe

2 cups all-purpose flour	½ cup shorting (solid
2 tsp. baking powder	Crisco, margarine)
1 tsp. salt	

Directions:

Place washed chicken pieces, and chicken stock in pot, add onion/celery/, and 2 tablespoons salt. Cook on medium/low heat, and simmer. Partially cover – cook 15 – 20 min. until chicken is tender.(optional) to thicken chicken and broth mixture, use 1/2 cup tap water mixed with 1 Tbs. cornstarch, or flour. Add a little at a time, and stir.

Dumplings: combine flour, baking powder and salt. Cut in shortening until crumbly; add milk to make a stiff dough. Roll out dough to about 1/8 inch thickness, and cut into long (1 to 1½") strips. Then, cut dough crossway into 1½"-2" strips. Dust lightly with flour, and drop one by one into boiling chicken and stock. Cover tightly with lid, and boil gently for 8 to 10 min.

Makes 15 – 20 servings

Chapter 17

After everyone had finished their sit-down picnic lunch, it was time for the last event of the day; the baseball game. The Deacons played against the layman. The deacons made sure they had at least ten men on the team just in case someone faltered, and he had to be replaced. They borrowed a few of the Deacons from two other churches. They were all in their thirties to mid–forties. The older deacons joined the rest of the crowd sitting around the perimeter on their stools and folding chairs. Some of the families spread out their picnic blankets and watched the game from where they were.

Connie was a bit worn out, and mighty fatigue when she got home. She laughed all over again thinking about the scene when Otis slid into third base, and Pastor Dixon called him out. The Deacons riled up strutting across the field from all sides trying to overthrow his decision. Then, the layman tried to tag the men out who left their bases because the umpire never called an official timeout. Arms and baseball caps were waving in the air. You could hear some of the discussion from across the field as each man tried to defend his point of view.
"Man, you must be blind!"
"I'm not blind. He was out!"
"Out! His foot was on the base for 'bout a half a minute before old Joe wobbled over there with the ball."

"Old! Who you calling old? And for your information I didn't wobble. I ran."

"Ran! Is that what you call running? Why I've seen babies crawl backwards faster than that."

Some of the men were laughing just as hard as the womenfolk. The friendly banter was comical. Everyone could tell that no one was really angry. The men had to have something to joke about on their way home that night. Otis took his defeat. Besides; everyone knew that Pastor Dixon's eyesight wasn't that great, and he was nearly blind when he wasn't wearing his glasses.

As sexy, and as handsome as Marcus thought he was, Connie was glad she turned down his offer to stop by the house and see her. He also asked for her telephone number a couple of times, and that was a definite – *No*. There wasn't any use inviting trouble. She was glad she got to Edmund before she left the picnic. She wanted to make sure he knew that Marcus was not to get her telephone number. It's no secret that he had a way with women. He was like that back in high school, and it looked like he hadn't changed much. He chased after anything in a skirt.

I felt sorry for some of the girls who thought *going all the way* with him would keep him as their steady, but it didn't. Two girls got pregnant by him, and one of the girls went to our church. It was such a great hurt and embarrassment to her and her family. Back in the mid-

50s that sort of reputation was not readily accepted by the church, your family, or even by the people in your neighborhood. She went to live with an aunt and uncle somewhere out of town.

I just hate that she never got a chance to graduate with our class. The other girl lived closer to the Atlanta area. It was rumored that her family had a little money, so they paid for her to get an abortion. That just wasn't a common thing for people in the *'Black'* community to do.

I feel a little differently now about some girls who aborted *'Seed'*. But back then I thought, *'serves them right for thinking they can go around ruining other people's lives and getting off scot-free'*. Regina's uncle and aunt ended up caring for the baby while she tried to finish school. Marcus didn't assume any responsibility for the baby at all, but how could he? He was a teenager himself. He wasn't responsible enough to do anything. I know people change, but from what I can see, he hadn't changed *that* much. He and his Mom lived with her mother. His father never married his mother.

The type of community we lived in back then were primarily two family households. There were very few single-parent households to speak of. By the time I was starting my second year of college, I heard that his mother had married and moved out of state with her new husband. That just left Marcus and his grandmother. Edmund said Marcus' grandmother passed away almost five years ago, and she left him the house they lived in over on Ridge Avenue, but little of anything else.

We all were entering, or had just entered our thirties about then. I guess it's fair to say that depending on what was instilled in you as a child, has a direct influence on what, or should I say who you became as an adult.

———

Connie was dressing for church, but couldn't get last night's dream out of her mind. She dreamt about the man's voice coming from behind her at the picnic table. In the dream she thought: *the man that handed me the lemonade wasn't Marcus, it was Otis.* That was very unusual for me, because one, I very seldom dream about a man and, two–if I did, his features are never sharp or clear. They are always a bit cloudy, and I never could quite make out who the person was. Connie slipped her feet into her high heel shoes and went over to the floor length mirror to check everything out.

In the dream she actually sat next to Otis at the table, but then the bench somehow turned into the two of them riding along at night in a car. He put his arm around her, and she leaned her head on his shoulder. Just before the dream ended, they were standing at her front door. He was leaning in to give her a kiss, and then she woke up.

Connie was having cold cereal and toast for breakfast, so she didn't worry about putting her robe on, or wrapping her hair. The volume on the hi-fi was turned up high. She did that purposely, hoping to drown out the thoughts that were running through her head. That was the closest she had come to being kissed (*at least in that way*) for a little more than four years. Connie wanted to go to service, but she didn't want to sit there with a flushed face every time she looked at Otis on the pulpit.

Otis woke up with feelings he hadn't felt for a long, long time. Some of the feelings were physical, and some were otherwise. First he went to bed angry. He didn't know why he should have been so upset over yesterday's happenings. After all, Constance wasn't his girl. She used to be years ago, but now she was free to talk to whomever she pleased. He just wished it hadn't been Marcus.

Just when he was going to sit at her picnic table; *Marcus beat him to the punch. If I had only been a few seconds quicker,* he thought. He knew what he was feeling was jealousy, pure and simple! But, it wasn't just jealousy. His feelings were mixed with a sense of protectiveness for Connie. She didn't ask for it, but those feelings arose in him the moment he saw her again.

If he were to be totally honest with himself, those feelings never *really* left. He always blamed himself for messing up with what could have been a relationship that led both of them to the altar. If he had not listened to his friends, she might not have married that *no*-count husband of hers, and he surely would not have married that deceitful ex-wife of his.

Otis hobbled to the shower. Almost every muscle in his body ached. If he had only thought last night that he might be this sore in the morning, he would have soaked in a tub of hot water. Now he was paying for all those fancy moves like: jumping high in the air to catch a *'fly ball'*, sliding into third base with one leg extended, and gliding onto home plate with one arm extended to catch *'punts'*. He really put on a show for the ladies, especially one lady in particular, and now he was paying for it.

Otis wiped the steam from the mirror and took the bottle of rubbing alcohol from the medicine cabinet. "This is something else I should have done last night, he said aloud." He went back to the bedroom to dress for church.

He was sitting on the edge of the bed getting ready to put on his socks when a particular scene from last night's dream entered his mind. He hopped off the bed, and stumbled over to the hassock in front of the window. *Wow*! Man that was unexpected.

There was no use denying what he was trying to deny. He *had* dreamt that! It is bad enough he thought, that that sort of thing would creep into my dreams. Of course, I'd expect that if we were married. But were we married in the dream? He wasn't sure. Dreams are funny that way. But, nonetheless, he had to clear his head, and purify his thoughts before he reached the house of God.

This wasn't the first time he had dreamt about Connie, but this surely was the first time the dream had gone *that* far. As far as he knew, Connie deserved the respect of a Christian lady, and he was going to see that she got it; even in his dreams.

So, being aware of the enemy's ploys he wasn't about to be overtaken by him. He finished dressing and grabbed his Bible. *From where I'm positioned most Sundays, it's hard not to take in the view of the whole audience. I surely don't want to feel out of order every time my eyes fall on Connie.*

He had to find something to fortify my strength. He was praying as he flipped through the pages of the New Testament, and stopped when his eyes rested on the words in the book of Philippians chapter four, verse eight.

"Finally; brethern, whatsoever things are true, whatsoever things are honest, whatsoever things are just, whatsoever things are pure, whatsoever things are lovely, whatsoever things are of good report; if there be any virtue, and if there be any praise, think on these things."

The word *'virtue'* stuck out in my mind.

Chapter 18

Sunday's service was great. Everyone's spirit was still high from the picnic. It was also evident that while some spirits were high, more than one or two of the *'Brothers'* in the congregation were experiencing stiffer movements in their steps because by yesterday's game. It was very noticeable, but nothing was said about it until Pastor Dixon was at the podium welcoming the visitors. One of the papers he was reading from fell to the floor, and I jumped to the rescue.

However, when I bent down to pick the paper off the floor, a slight groan escaped my lips, and when I tried to stand up, the grown became louder. The congregation erupted in laughter, as did Rev. Dixon verbally alluding to the fact that none of us were as young and spry as we used to be. He said most of us found that out when we woke up this morning.

During the service Otis made eye contact with me a couple of times, but neither of us lingered there. Actually, I felt a little embarrassed. The dream may have ended before his lips met mine, but I already knew what it felt like to kiss Otis Delaney. I also knew that this *was not the time*, nor the place to entertain that thought.

I had already decided to rejoin St. James church this Sunday. That was something I knew I would do even before I left Nashville, but then it was almost out of duty, or obligation. *Now*, I felt a new excitement about joining. This wasn't the same old St. James church. This church was growing and moving forward in the Lord. I felt as though I could really get involved with some of the new programs.

When the invitation went out to those who needed salvation, or needed a church home, I stepped into the aisle. Levee and Earl stood and applauded along with the rest of the congregation. I don't know why I felt so emotional standing there at the altar. After all, I had planned to join. Except... *well*, except that it actually felt different when it happened. During the altar call Otis came down to stand directly behind Pastor Thornton.

Maybe it was just my imagination, but it seemed like he never took his eyes off of me. Since pastor Dixon had originally been my pastor, Pastor Thornton asked if he would come down from the pulpit to receive me as a member. Everyone at the altar gave each other a 'holy-hug', and a lady with a notepad in her hand took me to another room just down the hall from the sanctuary.

A few minutes later Olivia poked her head in the door. "Congratulations sis", she said. She had my purse and my Bible in one hand, and her Bible in the other. I was handed a "*Welcome to St. James CME church*" packet. Because she was feeling a little discomfort, Earl said Levee had going to get the car. She wasn't going to linger around. She thought she would go home and put her feet up before dinner. Backing out through the door, she reminded me I always had an open invitation for

Sunday dinner at her house.

I finished filling out the information needed on the form and handed it back to the attendant. She hugged me again and said welcome to the kingdom of God, and to St. James church. She asked if there was anything else she needed to assist me with. I told her no, I would be just fine. She opened the door saying ordinarily she would take me back into service, but it seemed like the morning service had ended. As I gathered my things my mind turned towards Levee. I stepped into the hallway and Otis was leaning against the wall opposite the room I was in. I was surprised, but please. My puzzled look must have initiated an explanation from him.

"Welcome back, sister *Web*...Black."

I gave a light smile, and said Thank You. He said the formal part of in-take was over, that in the past when someone renewed their membership, they would be offered the '*right-hand*' of fellowship right there at the altar, but the congregation had grown so over the last few years, it became a time consuming ordeal to have the whole congregation file around to shake their hand. So, just those clergy, and '*Five Fold*' ministers who were serving the pulpit did the honors. Otis cleared his throat, and told me he was waiting for me in a non-official capacity.

"I was wondering if you would like to go with me somewhere for a light lunch" I hated not to answer right away, but now that this would have been my second opportunity to say 'Yes' I did. I was concerned about Levee. Otis's voice broke through my musing.

"If you rather not… I know this is being forward of me. Maybe I should wait until you get used to being back home."
I could tell he felt a little embarrassed and maybe a little disappointed too.

"Oh no" I said, "It's not that. I mean I would not mind it at all. It's just that Levee left church not feeling so well, and I, well… I didn't know if I needed to check on her or not. You know, being the *big sister* and all."
Otis gave that wonderful understanding smile of his, and when I looked in his eyes I felt like a silly little schoolgirl. What was the matter with me? "Well, if she just left" he said, maybe she's not quite home yet. Were you planning on dropping by her house, or would you like to make a phone call to see if she's okay?"

I could hear a small voice inside my head saying, *don't blow it!* She has a husband, and a brother to see to her if she needs anything. "If you want to wait around another five minutes or so to be sure their home, we can use the phone in Pastor Thornton's office." "Okay. Thanks. That would be nice."

Almost everyone had left the building. It felt a little strange walking down an empty hallway in a church. I can't remember if I had ever done that before. Otis let me in the pastor's private office. He said to take as long as I needed. He was going to bring his car around from the side parking lot. He asked if I wanted to go to "*dinner – dinner*", or if I wanted to drive by the *Dairette*. I really had to think about it, because in the excitement of me joining church, and Levee not feeling well, I actually wasn't *that* hungry.

Levee was feeling better. She said she just hadn't fully rested from yesterday's activities. Even so, I felt an excuse coming over me not to accept the invitation from Otis. I had to make a decision. He was going to return any minute and I didn't know what to tell him. I heard a light tap at the door, and Otis came in. He wanted to know if all was well with my sister, and I told him yes. I was honest with him and said I really wasn't very hungry. He gave me that half-quirky grin of his and said; "Too much excitement, huh?"
"Yeah, I guess so."

"Well", he looked at me and said, "This is the problem we have. One, we have two vehicles. I not sure what you think about this, but one of us could leave our car here at the church, and ride together in the other person's car, but I don't suggest that…for *obvious* reasons." He started laughing, giving me a sideward glance, and I joined in. That's all it would take to get a rumor started. "On the other hand, he said, if we both took our cars and ended up at the Dairette, (he hunched his shoulders and raised his hands waist high in a questioning motion) we could each sit in our separate cars and eat, or one of us could hop in the other person's car."

He looked at me standing there in my floral summer dress and matching pastel heals. I opened my eyes wide, and he said, "*No, No*, I guess hopping is out of the question." Then, both of us started laughing again.

"I don't know about you, but I don't think I'm ready for the "*public*" thing with the whole town talking. Let me see, you're not very hungry, and I'm pert near starved to death. Soo… how does this sound? If I may invite myself over to your house, I'm sort of a private person and I take it that you are too. Maybe if you run along home first, and kick off your shoes, I'll go pick up a couple of pizzas. Do you still like cheese with Canadian bacon?" I told him yes. He said good and wondered if about half an hour would be okay. I said "Yes, that would be just fine."

Chapter 19

Driving the short distance home, Connie thought; *what if this is some kind of trick just to get me alone in my house*?

She began to get nervous about the whole situation. But, what could she do now? The voice inside her head said: *Stop dreaming up excuses. If this was Marcus, you'd have something to worry about!* There was no way to get in touch with Otis anyway, and she felt better about what she heard her spirit say.

Connie drove the car around to the side of the house, and parked it in front of the garage. She went through the inside back door to the bedroom and kicked off her shoes. She left them beside the bed, and slipped her feet into her slippers. As soon as she did that, she changed her mind. She didn't want to look *that* comfortable. Connie went to the closet and took out a pair of sandals that complemented one of the pastel colors in her dress. She took a quick gaze of her recent pedicure to make sure everything was still intact. It was, and then she rushed to do the ritual with the air-conditioner and the fans to make the house more comfortable. After that she went to the kitchen. There was Coke, iced tea, and fruit drink in the refrigerator. Those would have to do.

Otis wanted to make a quick run by his 'crib', but changed his mind because he didn't want to prolong the time. He already had one additional stop to make. He would make the pizza pickup after that. He thought of the many times he passed the Webster house. He never broke ties completely with Connie's family, even after they broke up. He had great respect for her parents, and would stop by every now and then just for a chat. They even invited him to dinner several times after his divorce to Belinda. They said they would just keep that little secret between the three of them, and evidently they did.

Connie felt a little awkward, and wasn't sure how to go about talking to a man who was interested in her. Maybe she should just think of him as another friend. She hadn't dated since she was dating her (now deceased husband) almost ten years ago.

Maybe I'm jumping the gun, she thought. *Who says he's interested in me in that way? He really had not indicated more than just friendship.* Still, she wasn't sure what the conversation would turn to, but she was sure she wasn't ready to talk about *when they used to date,* and why they broke up! If she ran out of things to talk about she would ask how certain high school friends were doing, and what ever happened to *this* person, or *that* teacher? Connie got the yearbook from the bookcase in the Parlor and put it on the living room coffee table.

Otis parked his vehicle in the driveway and rang the front doorbell with his elbow. On her way to answer the door, Connie felt a little guilty wishing he had parked on the side near the garage, or even around in the back. She immediately dismissed the thought that was trying to make her feel self-conscious about inviting a man over to her house. She opened the front door and was more and was more than surprised to see Otis loaded down with packages. She pushed the screen door open.

"What in heaven's name?" Otis had two pizza boxes, a large brown bag, and two small cartoons propped on top of the pizza boxes. "Well", he said carefully trying to balance everything as he eased sideways through the door, "I remembered how much you used to like Chinese food with your pizza, so I stopped by Imperial Gardens and picked up some shrimp fried rice, pork egg foo young, rice, and two egg rolls." Connie's mouth was hanging wide open, but she was speechless. He looked at her and said:
"Wait a minute. You do still eat Chinese food with your pizza don't you?"

All she could do was nod her head '*yes*' as he headed to the kitchen with the packages. Connie closed the door and scurried behind him, still in somewhat of a daze.
Otis lowered everything onto the table, and then shot both arms out in the air and did a little tap shuffle as he tilted his head to one side saying; "*Ta-dah*! Congratulations on rejoining Saint James church today."

He had such a warming smile on his face Connie didn't know if to fall into his out stretched arms, or if she was going to fall to the floor. She just stood there for a moment dumbfounded. He lowered his arms, and the smile on his face slowly turned into a questioning stare.

"Uh-oh, you don't eat Chinese food with your pizza anymore." Connie found her voice and said, "Yes, yes I do. I just find it very surprising that you remembered a little thing like that."

"There are a lot of things I remember about you."

It wasn't what he said. It was the way he said it. Connie felt like butterflies were circling in her stomach, and her knees felt weak, hopefully from the hunger that just came back over her. She slid my foot along the floor to feel for the chair and plopped herself down in it. She then put a little strength in her voice and said, "Well, what are we waiting for? Let's eat!"

Connie felt a sudden urge to serve his plate, but shook it off. Instead she said, "I guess this is self-service, so you go first."

After they both had selected their choices, she almost started to pick up her slices of pizza and take a bite out of it. She was extending her hand towards her plate, and when Otis saw the gesture, he extended his hand to meet hers, and said "Shall we pray?" Obviously misunderstanding her extended hand. So, as not to be embarrassed she reached across the table and placed her hands in his.

Lord, forgive me. I know this man must have said a nice grace, but after his hands locked around mine, I didn't hear a word he said. I could only hope that I didn't embarrass myself by not relinquishing his hands when the prayer was over.

The conversation was light and easy. Otis knew most of who was still around town, and who wasn't. He helped me put away the leftovers, and we moved from the kitchen into the living room. He shared just a little about his failed marriage, taking most of the blame.

I could sense it was a hurting moment in his life. I'm not sure why, because he didn't go into any of the particulars.

I found myself sharing some of the details surrounding my unhappy marriage, and things that led to my husband's death. I could tell he was surprised about my circumstances, and knowingly felt empathetic. I don't know why I shared some of those personal things with him. Up until then, only my Mom and my mother-in-law knew some of the things I went through in my marriage.

Otis said after his father died from a heart attack, his sister had his mother to move in with her and her family. When that happened, he and his mother didn't have Sunday dinners together like they all used to at her house. He was divorced, his dad had passed on, and his mom was living with his sister. Otis said he knew he could have gone over there any time he wanted to, but for some reason he felt like a *loner,* and an *outsider*; someone with no *real* family. As I listened to him, I knew exactly what he meant, because I had that same feeling many a day.

149

We had been talking for about half an hour or so, and I asked if I could get him something to drink, or if he cared for a cup of tea. He said tea sounded nice. I told him he could get comfortable (he still was wearing his tie from the morning's service), and I would be right back.

Otis took off his tie, undid the top button on his collar, and roll up the cuffs of his sleeves. Feeling a little more relaxed, he looked around the familiar living room and noticed a few changes. His eyes fell once more on the high school yearbook laying the coffee table. He smiled as he reached for it. He looked at the year etched on its cover and thought, *Man has it been that long?*

Connie returned with two cups of warm tea. Otis took a sip from his cup.

"Umm, looks like I'm not the only one who remembers people's *likes* from the past. This tea is perfect. It's not too hot, and it's sweetened just the way I like it."

Connie didn't know what to say, so she just said, "Thank you." She hadn't really thought about it, because when they first started dating she always made her hot tea the way her mother made it. But, he was right. When they began to date, Connie made a cup of hot tea for him the way her mother always made it for her; flavoring it with two teaspoons of sugar and evaporated canned milk.

Now she remembered it was Otis who first had her to make his tea with two tablespoons of honey, and freshly squeezed lemon. She liked it so much she began making it that way for herself from then on. She even remembered not to make it so hot, that you had to blow over the surface several times just to get a sip. Oh, she made it warm enough to drink, but not so hot that you had to wait forever for it to cool down.

They looked through the yearbook laughing at the way they looked in high school, and pointed out who liked who before the two of them started dating each other. Of course, Marcus Yancey's name came up. Otis made a comment about him showing up at the church picnic, and under his breath said, "*Ruining everything.*" But she heard it.

It made me feel good to know that Otis was a little jealous of that incident. Oh, not in a vindictive way. It just made me feel a little special.

I haven't had someone to feel jealous over me for a long time, and that included my late husband. Otis said he didn't have to open his shop on tomorrow because of the Labor Day holiday. He also said he didn't want to seem presumptuous, or to impose on me, but if I wanted the company, he could stay for a while longer.

I wanted the company!

Brownie Surprise

Preheat oven 375°

1½ cup flour
¼ tsp baking powder
1¾ cup sugar
2 eggs
½ cup melted butter
1 cup crushed peppermint candy
1 bark of sweet chocolate 16 oz.
½ tsp salt
¼ tsp pumpkin spice, or
½ tsp grated nutmeg

Directions: Mix dry ingredients and set aside.
Fill a large cooking pot ½ full with water, bring to a boil, remove from stove. Place large glass mixing bowl inside pot of hot water. Do not let water overspill into glass bowl. Put bark of chocolate in bowl and stir with wooden spoon until melted. Blend in melted butter and eggs (one at a time). Stir in dry ingredients a little at a time. Mixture should be spreadable, but not a thick dough. Add crushed peppermint candy, stir. Spread mixture in a 13x9 baking pan. Bake 12-15 minutes. Let cool completely before cutting into squares. Serve.

Chapter 20

Otis called on Monday to say how much he enjoyed his visit. The night before, we ended up watching a couple of Sunday evening TV shows: 'Wild Kingdom', and the *'Leslie Uggams Show'*. I used the microwave to reheat some slices of pizza, and the egg rolls. I guess I was feeling more relaxed and comfortable around him, so much so, that I didn't have sense enough to call it a day– *but* he did.

He said he didn't want the neighbors counting down the hours of his visit. Besides that, he said he was still a little bit stiff from yesterday's activities and wanted to get home to soak his sore muscles in a *tub* of hot water. I was feeling so drawn to him by then, I could have offered him mine.

Actually, it wasn't until he left, and I was sitting there alone that I realized how much I miss having someone to talk to. I guess up until a couple of months ago I was preoccupied with my full-time job, visiting my mother-in-law, and participating in a few church activities. The rude awakening is that I must have been lonely, or longed for companionship even then. It's just that I filled the empty moments with all of the other stuff I was doing.

As a matter of fact, church was hard to do; not because the people weren't kind and loving, but because they were. It was the sitting alone, and seeing husbands and wives sitting together. Sometimes a husband would unconsciously stretch his arm across the back of the pew encircling his wife's shoulder. It was a very normal thing for couples to do, but for someone who had just been divorced, or widowed, it brought on an instant pang of being alone. Of course, everyone is different, but that was one of the things that was challenging for me to overcome. I even stopped watching romantic, love movies.

Otis wanted to know if I had anything planned for the day. I told him no. He said if I was *gamed*, he would like to take me to the amusement park just on the outskirts of Atlanta. It was completed during the years I still lived in Nashville. I told him I wasn't much for large roller coasters, and rides that made you feel like the bottom of your stomach was dropping out. I would love to go.

I knew the weather was going to be pretty mild, somewhere in the mid-eighties, but depending on when we left and when we were to return, the evenings could get a little cool. I thought that whatever I wore I would be sure to take a sweater along with me. Otis said he wanted to wait until early evening to pick me up, mainly because he knew the park would be full of parents and their kids getting in their last fling of summer before starting school on Tuesday.

For the outing I pulled my hair back in a ponytail and fastened it with a barrette. I wore another one of my pedal– pusher outfits, but this time with a pair of *"Flat-ties"*.

I had a fetish about getting sand or dirt on my bare toes. I didn't feel the need to carry a big pocketbook, so I got out my change purse, put my driver's license, door key, and a $10 bill in it. I put the change purse in one of my front pockets. The other pocket was for my tube of lipstick and a couple of breath mints.

I tried to go about the rest of my day in a normal manner, but I kept being interrupted by my nerves. I called my mother-in-law. I could feel I was calling her less and less, so I talked to her for about twenty, or thirty minutes. After I hung up from her, I called Levee to see what they were going to do for the weekend. Of course Edmund was coming over for the little family cookout, and I was invited too.

When I gave her my excuse for why I wouldn't be there, she exploded with glee. I had to ask her not to put more into this outing then what it really was–*a casual outing* with a mutual old acquaintance. And, I had to emphasize that '*mum*' was the word, and to please, please, *please* keep this between the two of us until I knew for myself where *this* was going.

Otis told himself he was just being ridiculous. He must've tried on four or five combinations of different shirts and pants before he finally decided on what he was going to wear. He had to laugh at himself, because he thought only women did this. It was a good thing he had already had his hair cut two days ago, because all the barbershops he knew of were closed today. Most of them were closed on Mondays anyway. He had to calm himself down. He cut himself shaving, and he burnt his breakfast. *Sure,* he said to himself, *you were' Joe Cool' when you were asking her out on the phone, but look at you now. You're a nervous wreck!* The best thing to do right then was to pray.

"Father, I know I'm a man. You made me that way. But, I'm a Godly man, and I don't need my flesh rising up to defeat the chance I've been waiting for. I messed things up almost fourteen years ago, and now You have bought this woman back into my life again. I can't blow it this time. I know I'm a man of moral character, and Constance is a woman of integrity. I walk according to the Spirit, and not according to the flesh. Maybe I ought to say that again Lord. *I walk according to the Spirit, and not according to the flesh.* I love you God, and I believe that I never stopped loving this woman. Please, help me to be a man-a friend she can depend on and trust, in Jesus' name, Amen.

Otis got up from his knees, and sat on the edge of the bed. He smiled to himself when he realized he got up with ease. His soreness was gone. He looked up to the ceiling and said: "Thank you Lord! I sure didn't want to hobble around like an old man on this first date with Connie."

He thought about getting dressed, but still felt he had a lot of built-up nervous energy. Aside from that, he had four more hours before his date. *How am I going to fill them,* he thought? "My car", he said aloud. "I can't pick Connie up in that dirty car." He went down to the

garage and backed the car out into the driveway. His pickup truck was parked on the street, so he didn't have to worry about moving a second vehicle. He got the bucket, sponge, some rags, and turned
on the garden hose.

This should take about an hour. I'll have to dry the car off, and clean the inside. Thank goodness it already had a wax job about four weeks ago. It still looks pretty good!

When he finished with his car, Otis drove it down to the gas station on Redan Street to fill it up with gas. He didn't want to do it later on, and chance smelling like fuel on his date. He bought a pack of chewing gum, (*one of the bad habits he had*) bad because it pulled out one of his fillings. He put the gum back, and bought a candy bar.

When Connie opened the door, Otis gave an admiring eye of her appearance, saying how nice she looked. She thanked him, and thought to herself...*You don't look half bad yourself.* Otis walked beside her, and caught a whiff of her fragrant perfume in the warm summer breeze. It was light, but intoxicating.

He opened the passenger front door, and with her feet still planted on the ground she sat on the seat, and then she lifted both legs at the same time, then turning her body and brought her feet to rest on the floor mat in front of her. Just that little gesture of femininity caused
a stir of excitement in Otis. It let him know all the more that he was dealing with a lady of class, and character.

Connie took in a quick glance of the interior. *Hum, nice,* she thought. *You can tell a lot about a man by the way he keeps his car, and from the looks of this, I would say he is clean-cut, attentive, and caring.*

Their conversation on the way out of town was upbeat and interesting. Otis talked about the church, and his new business. Connie found out that Otis had gone to the Air Force after his divorce, and went to a technical college when he came back home. Evidently, his knowledge of masonry and carpentry, along with what he learned in electronics, was very helpful to him when he decided to go into business for himself.

Connie thought maybe he could be the person to ask about making another entry way for the downstairs bathroom. But, she wouldn't ask him right now, she would wait until later. For right now she leaned her back against the soft leather seat enjoying the hum of Otis' voice, and took in the pleasant aroma of peppermint, and 'Old Spice'.

Chapter 21

It seems like both of us were being cautious about keeping this outing as *just* old friends getting together. When the evening began, we were very careful not to be so familiar as to hold hands with each other. We were trying to be our natural selves, but somehow it seemed to put a strain on the outing. Otis was such a gentleman, stepping to one side and waving me in front of him whenever we got near a gate to pay for the tickets. I told him one of my favorite rides was the *Tilt- A-Whirl*. In some amusement parks they call it *The Whip*, because it whipped you around in a circle during certain parts of the ride, and then it reverses and swings you in the other direction.

Several times the ride tilted and turned so fast it caused us to push together on one side of the seat. The centrifugal force caused our bodies to press against each other. I held onto the bar and squealed several times during the ride. When the ride ended, I started to lift the bar and get out of my seat, but Otis stopped me.

"Hey, where do you think you're going?" "The ride is over isn't it?"

"Not for us. You said this was one of your favorite rides, so I paid for us to ride two times."

Now, I was a little embarrassed because it had been so many years since I had ridden on this particular ride, I had forgotten how it pinned you against each other with its forceful whips. Then, I thought, *what if he thinks I wanted to ride this ride just for that reason*? I spoke up and said:

"I picked this ride because it was at ground level. I forgot how jerky and forceful it was."

"That's okay. I haven't ridden it for years myself. If it gets too much for you to handle the second time around (he gave a small chuckle), I'll be right here to help—unless you really would rather get off now." Before I could say anything, the attendant must have collected tickets from all of the other new riders, and the gears started rolling. We looked at each other, laughed, and shrugged our shoulders as if to *say: Oh well, it's too late now I guess we're in for the second time around.*

This time around when the ride forced me against his arm, he still held on to the lift bar. But, the second time the ride pinned me against him, Otis lifted one of his hands from its grip on the bar, and put it around my shoulders. I tried not to flinch. My stomach did a few flip-flops, but I didn't look at him until the ride was almost over. When it stopped our seat was sitting on an upslope, so our seat whirled around on its own a few more times before it came to a complete stand still.

By that time, I was feeling woozy. The ride had stopped, but my head kept going around, and around. I tried to stand, but my legs felt weird. I was looking straight ahead of me, but my body was veering to the right. Suddenly I felt a strong arm encircled my waist, and a hand gripped mine. I could feel myself leaning against the left side of Otis's body.

Then he was saying something in my ear. He smelled of *Old Spice*, and peppermint.

"Whoa. You're walking wobbly. You better let me help you off the ride. Maybe we should not have taken that second turn around, but it was too late for us to get off."

Otis felt guilty that the ride made Connie a little woozy, but was pleased that it gave him a chance to put his arm around her again. And now, to actually be holding her in his arms while they walked off the ride was more than he had hoped for.

Connie head was foggy. She wasn't sure if she was reeling from the ride, or from being that near to Otis. They stood for a few minutes so she could collect herself, and Otis asked if she was feeling better. Connie wanted to say 'no', but she knew she would be lying. A little voice in her head said: *Go ahead and lie, go ahead and lie!* While another one in her heart said: *Be honest.*

"Well, I think I'm okay, but to tell you the truth, I would feel a little more secure if you continue to support me until we got to that bench over there." She pointed to the empty part bench under a big shade tree. Connie knew she probably could have walked to the bench on her own, but she thought, *what the heck, I want to prolong the moment and I did not tell a lie.*

Otis tried not to let his eagerness to accommodate her show on his face. But, he had to look down at his feet to make sure they were walking normal, and not doing a jig.

———

Connie stayed seated while Otis went to get them a Chicago style hot dogs, funnel cakes, a 7up, and a Coke.

Otis returned, doing a balancing act with the funnel cakes and the drinks. He had a folded bag gripped between his teeth. Connie caught the bag in mid-air just as it slipped from his teeth into her hand. He moved his mouth and chin back and forth several times. When he sat on the bench he placed the drinks and funnel cakes between the two of them. Then he quickly raised his hands to his jaws, and rubbed each side of his face. Connie felt badly that he had to carry the hot dog bag in his teeth.

He told her that everything came from a different vendor stand, and nobody wanted to give him a bag. Otis said he had to ask for the drink holder, explaining to the man that he had a ways to walk. He then said it probably wouldn't have taken as long as it did, but he forgot which tree he left me sitting under. It really wasn't funny, but I did get tickled as I imagined him wandering around the park lost, and unable to speak. When we finished eating, we went on another ride or two (no loop- d-loops), and then headed for the parking lot. Otis had to open his shop the next morning, so we drove directly back to my house.

Connie was thinking, and she knew the *'good nights'* were always awkward to handle on the first date, even for people their age. Luckily, before they came up to her driveway Otis asked if he could go in and use the restroom. She went to the restroom once while they were at the park, but she wasn't sure if Otis had gone or not, because he was standing outside of the ladies' restroom waiting for her. He said he just wanted to make sure she was safe.

Connie let both of them into the house, and went through to turn on the kitchen light. Otis knew the house well enough to remember that the downstairs bathroom was through the kitchen. Connie thought it would be embarrassing standing around waiting for a man to come out of the bathroom, so she went back out through the front door and sat on the porch swing. It was only about 8:30 pm. The day was just drifting into twilight time.

Connie stood up when Otis came through the front door. "Oh, you don't have to get up." He strolled across the porch. In order to avoid and awkward situation, because Connie didn't know what he had in mind she nervously said, "Do you want to sit with me on the porch swing for a while?" "Sure. Why not? I've got a few minutes before I have to go."

Otis was glad for the offer, because he wasn't quite sure how to say good night. The thing that ran through both of their minds that *neither one of them dared to mention*, was the way they used to sit on that very swing and '*neck*' when they were dating. Connie broke into their silence.

"Thanks again for asking me to go with you today. I had a wonderful time." "Well, you're more than welcome. It was my pleasure. Things can get a little monotonous when your single and live alone. You know… doing the same-o, same-o. He caught himself and said: Oh, I was talking about me, not you."

"No, that's alright, but I thought it was different for you guys. You all can go places and do things alone, and no one would think anything of it. The moment a young lady does the same thing, everybody thinks she's after something, or someone."

"I know. It is unfair. But, just because a guy can go here, there, and yonder by himself it doesn't mean he enjoys going there alone. Trust me a man would like it much better if he had someone to go along with him, preferably a lady." "Well, I guess you're right. But, somehow I thought it was only us girls who felt that way." Connie could see the conversation was making a shift, so before Otis could lead into something she was not ready for, she changed the subject.

"Hey, Otis how much carpentry, and plumbing do you actually know?" "I know a little bit about what I'm doing. I'm not a professional or anything like that. Why do you ask?"

"You know the bathroom you just used?"
"Yeah."
"Well, I was wondering if there was a way to make it accessible from my parent's bedroom… I mean my

bedroom, without going all the way down the hall, and through the kitchen."

Otis felt a flush of awkwardness come over him just thinking about entering Connie's bedroom. He shook it off, and tried not to look directly into her eyes.
"I don't know. I'd have to see how everything is laid out before I could make any kind of evaluation. When are you thinking about having that done?"
"Pretty soon I guess. Oh, I don't mean for you to go and look at it now, but do you think you could stop around Tuesday after you close your shop? I think I know what I want, but I'll need some advice to see if it's feasible."

Just that quickly, twilight had turned to dusk. Otis stood to his feet, and Connie stood too.
"I guess I'd better say good night."

Now he was stuck. He knew a kiss was definitely out of order, and a handshake would make him look like he was '*square*'.

Then he thought, a Holy-hug is always in order. Otis stepped closer to Connie, putting his right arm lightly around the back of her shoulder. He kept his left arm at his side. Then, he bent his head down so the side of his face was on the side of hers, and kissed into the air. He said "good-night", making sure his lips did not touch her face. In that quick moment his nostrils breathed in the faintness of her perfume.

He immediately released his arm; not realizing 'til then, that Connie had performed this same gesture toward him. Otis walked quickly to his car. He waved goodbye again, hopped in the car, and put the gears in to reverse.

Chapter 22

After Otis's car was out of sight, Connie went back and sat on the porch swing. "*Sister*" she said aloud, "you've got some serious praying to do." She thought about how she had planned the way she thought she would live for a while when she got back home. But, things didn't seem to be flowing in that direction.

Her plan was to float for about three months until she was use to the old community again. Then, she was going to get a job–although she wasn't sure if she wanted to do the same thing she had been doing, and then maybe in a couple of years she would meet a nice guy and they would start dating. Those were her plans; except that one little thing happened. *A fly showed up in the ointment.* His name was Otis Delaney!

Her plans were already thwarted. Connie had to smile to herself when the thought of one of her father's familiar scriptures came up in her spirit.

"Many *plans* are in a man's heart, but the counsel of the Lord will prevail."

The Scripture brought back fond memories of her dad, but also caused her to question why that particular Scripture in Proverbs would come up *at this* particular time?

Otis knew he was in trouble. On the drive home, his thoughts were *everywhere*. He almost ran a red light. *(well he actually did run the light).* He couldn't understand it. He prayed for strength' yet his flesh was stirred. *That's stupid*, he thought. *You stayed within the parameters you set for yourself; and yet a Holy-hug threw you completely off balance.*

Otis left the car parked in the driveway, and went in the front door. He quickly ran down the hall, stopping at the bathroom. He had to get a *good* look at himself in the mirror. He had to see if he looked as frazzled as he felt. *He did.*

"Alright!" He spoke to the guy in the mirror. "Get a grip on yourself. Pull yourself together. You put out the *chase,* and you made the first move."

Otis paced the floor a couple of times, and came back to the sink. He threw both hands palms down on the counter. He looked in the mirror again, and said; "Okay... okay, admit it. You're afraid." He was, and he quoted 2Timothy 1:7: "For God has not given us a spirit of fear, but of power and of love and a strong mind."

The evening was dwindling on, and he knew he had to open his shop in the morning. The day had been long, and he needed to take a shower. Otis thought, *that's what I need. Power and a strong mind. Cause right about now; my flesh is weakening thinking about the word love in that verse, and I'm not thinking about it in a 'brotherly' way. Maybe what I need to do is to take a cool shower.*

Otis lathered up, and tried his best to focus his mind on things of God. He rinsed off, and reached for the shampoo. Adjusting the temperature of the water from cool to warm, he squeezed the shampoo directly from the bottle onto his head. The warmer water began to relax his nerves. Before he knew it, he was singing a song that played on the car radio on the way back home. "*Sugar pie honey bunch, you know that I love you. I can't help myself. I love you and nobody else.*"

Suddenly, a voice (somewhat verbal) entered his hearing and said, "I have answered your prayer. She *is* your wife."
Otis froze in his tracks. He was so overwhelmed, that all he could do was stand there and let the falling, warm water run down his face to mingle with his tears.

Streaks of oranges and greys disappeared from the evening sky as dust turned into night. Connie got up from the porch swing, and took another glance at the sky before going into the house. She locked the front door, turned on the floor lamp in the Parlor, and went to the kitchen. She ran a glass of tap water and it took a few sips from the glass. Wanting to use the bathroom, she set the glass on the kitchen counter and started towards the door.

Connie was almost ready to go in, and stopped just short of walking through the door. Knowing that Otis was the last one to use this restroom, she felt a flush of embarrassment come over her. It was silly, but she was actually blushing about going in the bathroom after his presence had been in that private space.

171

"On second thought, she said aloud, I think a nice soak in the tub would make me feel better." She made a U-turn, and went to her bedroom.

While she was in the bedroom gathering her things to take upstairs, the telephone rang. Connie just knew it had to be Levee wanting to find out how things went on her date with Otis, even though she wasn't calling it a date. It was just an outing between old friends. She reached for the *princess* phone on the nightstand.
"Hello".
It wasn't Levee. It was a man's voice, and it didn't belong to Otis Delaney.
"Hey pretty lady. What's a doll like you doing out so late?"

At first she thought it was an obscene phone call, but then she recognized the voice. Connie was so annoyed at his disrespectful greeting that she didn't respond to it at all. How in the world did Marcus get this number?

"I called a couple of times this evening hoping to catch you in so I could drop by your 'crib', you know for a little high school reunion, but I guess you were out. Don't tell me you started staying out past your curfew?" Connie thought as she listened to his jargon; *here is one poor fool who hasn't grown up since high school, and besides that, he's living in a time-warp!*

"Excuse me. How did you get my number?"
"It wasn't that hard to get *Baby*. I know a couple of 'cuties' who work at the phone company."

"What! You mean to tell me that somebody gave you my number before it came out in the telephone book? Isn't that illegal, or something?"

"Hey, hey wait a minute *doll*. They didn't do anything illegal. First of all, I gave them your name and address. You're already listed in their system. So, all I had to do was give them my information like you do when you call the operator. Then, they gave me your number. What's the big deal?"

The big deal! The big deal is that…is that…Connie was so upset she couldn't think of what she wanted to say.

"Look, Marcus said, you're already listed. If you weren't, they wouldn't have been able to give me your number. I guess you don't have a *private* number. Anyway, the phone books will be out in about three more weeks."

"Okay Marcus, let me say this in a nice way. We may have gone to the same high school, and we may have been in some of the same classes, but we *never* have been what you call *friends*."

"Oh, still "*Miss uppity*" I see."

"Marcus, look. There's nothing wrong with people having their *own* preference of friends. It's still a free country. You had your group of friends that you ran around with in High school, and I had mine. Let me put it this way. I'm a Christian lady, and I have always gone to church, and well…that never seemed to be one of your interests back then, and from what I can tell, it's not one of yours now. I'm sure you only came to the picnic because you were in the parade with my brother, and he probably told you I was back in town and was going to be there. Well, to be honest… I'm just not interested in hanging out with the *Old gang,* and doing high school stuff."

"What jah mean by that? What are you trying to say?"

"Marcus, it's been fourteen years since high school. We all have made different choices in life, and we all have made some mistakes. Look, I've got an idea. Why don't you come to church this Sunday? I'm sure if you come…"

Marcus cut her off in mid-sentence.
"Yeah, yeah. I didn't call you to listen to all *that* church and Jesus stuff."

"Well, I'm sorry to hear that, because that's all I can give you. There's going to come a time when you might need to call on the name of the Lord, and…"

"Yeah, but that time's not now, and if that's *all* you're about, nobody needs your *prissy, self-righteous* old self anyway."

Before Connie could say anything else, she heard a click on the line, and then dial tone. She slowly put the receiver back on its cradle. Those last words he said stung. They sent hurting darts to her heart. *Isn't that just like the devil,* she thought; *just when your spirit is glowing with hope, and expectancy, he throws a stumbling block in your path.*

Baked Glazed Ham

7-10 lb. pre-cooked Ham
½ cup clear Karo syrup
¼ cup pineapple juice
½ cup brown sugar
¼ cup cherry juice
Wooden tooth picks
1 can pineapple ring 16oz
1 jar whole maraschino cherries
½ cup granulated sugar

DIRECTIONS: Pre-heat oven to 325°. Rinse ham, and place in shallow rack pan, or roaster pan. Fix pineapple rings close together on top and sides of ham with tooth picks pushed half way down. Fasten cherries to ham either inside the pineapple ring, or between the diamond shapes formed by the outer edge of the pineapples. Cover with foil. Bake 1½ to 2 hours.

SAUCE: In small sauce pan blend together brown sugar, granulated sugar, Karo syrup, the pineapple and cherry juice. Cook over medium to low heat, stirring often until mixture thickens. Cook for about ½ hour until glaze forms. Uncover ham, and baste every 5-10 min. until mixture is finished. Cook the ham another 7-10 minutes longer. Remove from oven, and let stand 10-15 minutes before slicing.

Chapter 23

Connie bathed and came down to her room. She imagine why people thought she was so lucky to be single.

It has its advantages, but for the most part, there is a lot of alone time. There is no one there to personally pour your heart out to. No one to share with at the end of a long trying day, and no one to let you know that, *'everything's going to be all right'*.

She could call Levee, but Connie knew she would have been in bed an hour ago. Her parents were no longer around. It seemed the Lord was pulling her away from her mother-in- law, and she had only joined the church a couple of days ago. There was no one to call on but the Lord. Connie knelt down beside her bed and began to pray.

"Dear Lord, You are the only one I can talk to now. You know the burden that is in my heart. All I know is that You have set a standard for me, and I won't accept anything less. I messed up once before in this area, and I don't want to mess it up again. The first thing I want to do is to ask Your forgiveness for the way I spoke to Marcus. I ask You to send the Comforter, and the ministering angels to remove the sting of hurting words from my spirit. I love You Lord. Keep me, and uphold me by the power of Your Word. Take control over my thoughts and my dreams, in Jesus' name. .Amen."

Otis knew he had to be dreaming. He woke up in a sweat. His heart was pounding. Beads of sweat danced across his forehead, and trickle down the sides of his face. He sat straight up in the bed. "What the heck?"
He knew he wasn't the type of man to be fist fighting anyone, yet in the dream he was physically boxing someone, and he was not playing around with it either.

The dream started with him and Connie at the amusement Park, and then all of a sudden, he was running down her street chasing after someone. Connie was sitting on her front porch in the swing. He chased whoever it was right into her driveway. The next thing he knew, he was being overpowered by the figure, and then Connie stood up and threw him a big Bible.
Then, the person in the dream became a shadow, and he beat the shadow over the head with the Bible.
The shadow disappeared, and the scene switched to the movie "*To Sir with Love*". But in the dream, it was Constance singing the song "To Sir with Love" to him, instead of the original performer, Lulu. When she got close enough for him to reach out and touch her, Pastor Dixon appeared between them. He picked the Bible up from the ground and said, "I'm her protector."

He woke up leaving both of them standing there looking at Pastor Dixon.

Otis didn't know what to think. He looked at the alarm clock on the nightstand, in seeing the time, he realized it was too late to try and get any more sleep, so he got up to start his day.

———————

Olivia was anxious to hear about Connie's date. She finished her morning routine of preparing breakfast, and getting her husband off to work. Today was going to be a little more relaxing. She would be home alone. On his way to work her husband was dropping off Earl Jr. by the grandparent's house. Olivia had not had much time to talk with her sister since she returned, and she really wanted to go by the house for a visit. There was just something about sitting and talking in Mama's kitchen that brought her comfort. She used to do it often when her mother was alive. Every now and then a melancholy moment would come over her, and this was one of those times. She called her sister (who sounded as if she'd just woke up) and asked if she could come over for a visit. To Connie, her prayer had been answered, and she suggested that Levee come over for lunch.

The sisters talked and shared with each other. They went over fond memories of growing up and living with their parents right there in that house. Of course, it set off a spurt of sadness, but it soon lifted. They shared with each other how they both found themselves doing, and saying some of the very things their parents used to do and say. Levee was helping Connie wash the dishes after lunch, when the telephone rang.

The thought of Marcus calling back to harass her jumped into her mind, and she tried to speak normally when she asked her sister to answer the phone. But as soon as she headed for the phone, Connie thought, *what if it's Otis?* It was too late. Her sister reached for the receiver before Connie could stop her. Well, whoever was on the other end, Levee knew them. Olivia said a few comments back and forth to the listener. Connie wasn't trying to eavesdrop, but was relieved when she realized Olivia was talking to her husband.

Levee said he called to remind her to check in on Earl Jr. at the grandparents. She said he was laughing when he said he knew how chatty sisters could be when they got together.

With all the talking they did, Connie left the subject of Otis as being only a friendly acquaintance. Olivia left about three o'clock. She had to stop by the grocery store on the way home. She told me she had to pick up some kind of spice I never heard of to put in some special dish she wanted to prepare for dinner. As was afore mentioned, she is the creative one in the family when he comes to the culinary department. That's one of the things from Mama that didn't rub off on me.

Otis had to play catch-up the next day when he reopened his shop. Usually Mondays were slow for pickups, so it was a great day for starting on new repairs.

But since it was Tuesday, he was a day behind. He kept busy enough, but his thoughts kept drifting between his date with Connie, and last night's dream. He had an urge to telephone her, but kept putting it off because he didn't know what to say even if he did call. He thought, *you just can't call somebody for no reason.* Yet, he knew one of the reasons was that he wanted to hear her voice. Apart from that, he wanted to see her face, to smell her perfume, and most of all, to hold her in his arms again.

The day passed on, and Otis must have reached for the telephone a half dozen times. Each time he thought, *what are you going to say?* He resolved that maybe calling her the next day after their outing was not such a good idea. Maybe it would make him seem to anxious. He didn't want to pressure her, but he *did* want to pursue.

Otis resolved that he would see Connie at Bible study on Wednesday night. He kept the shop open an hour later just in case some vacationing customer needed to drop something off. He didn't feel like going straight home, so he stopped by the Dairette for a double hamburger, onion rings, and a chocolate milkshake. He didn't eat like that often, but tonight he just felt like it!

Otis fiddled around the house for a while, and then he turned on the TV to listen to the late news. The investigation was ongoing concerning the Alaska Airline flight that crashed into the side of the mountain near Juneau, Alaska. The reporter said the Boeing 727 that went down on Saturday, September 4th killed all 111 people on board. Otis's heart was filled with compassion for the family and their loved ones. Here he was having a good time at the church picnic, and had gone through Sunday and Monday without listening to any news.

He felt a little guilty because he knew his thoughts were pretty much occupied with himself and Constance Black. He sat for a moment asking God for forgiveness, and to pray for the victims and their family. There was something also about the U.S. Ping-Pong team visiting Beijing, but after that his mind floated away from the news… And back to Connie.

Otis was in bed, and was drifting off to sleep when something Connie mentioned to him came back to mind. He opened his eyes and a smile creviced his face. "That's it", he said. "That's it! Thank you Jesus! Connie said something about wanting me to look at her bathroom to see if a second entry way could be made from her bedroom." Otis smiled even broader. *Hum,* he thought, *that's the reason I need to call her tomorrow.* "Lord, you are A-OK.!

I can call her from work in the morning, plus I'll get a chance to see her tomorrow night at Bible study. "Thanks Lord, You really know how to hook a '*brother*' up.

Chapter 24

Connie woke up not in the best of spirits. She moped around the house in her bathrobe and slippers. Her breakfast was brown, and just as bland as she felt: cornflakes, wheat toast with peanut butter, and a cup of applesauce. She knew it was her own fault. Had she pushed Otis away? "Maybe I was too stand-offish. Should I have called him yesterday?"

Connie fixed herself a cup of instant coffee, and went out front to get the morning paper. Just then Mrs. Miller was passing by the house. She went for a walk almost every day, and most evenings. She told me it was to help keep up her health, but I think it was to help keep up her gossip. I waved and quickly turned back to go into the house. I'm sorry. I just didn't feel like talking to anyone today.

Connie thumbed through the newspaper not really looking for anything in particular. Although she thought she was going to look in the 'Want Ads ' for a job.

It was already late morning, so Connie decided to wash up, and put on some clothes. It had been a couple of weeks since the grass was cut. Maybe she would call Edmund to see if he could come this Saturday to cut the grass. In the meantime, she gathered up a few things for the laundry and took them to the garage. Connie dropped the towels and other linens in the laundry basket beside the washer and dryer. *Humm,* she thought, that was another blessing that came to her parents from the Styles.

Most families *black*, or *white* had to use the local Laundromats. Connie couldn't remember if at that time her mother was still working for the Mayor's family or not, but they always did whatever they could to make our family's life easier. They even had a professional company to come and do whatever it took to install the washer and dryer correctly. The set was only about five years old when they gave it to us, and it still ran just as good today.

Connie heard the telephone rang, and dashed from the garage to the bedroom to answer it. She got it just on the last ring. Usually Edmund called when she was thinking about calling him, and when she answered the phone she almost said, "I was just thinking about calling you", but instead she said: "Hello." It was a good thing she didn't go through with her first thought, because it was Otis.

"Hello Constance, how are you doing?"

"I'm fine Otis, how are you?"

There was a pause on the line, and it seemed that neither one of us knew what to say past that. She heard Otis clear his throat and then he said, "Hey, you recognize my voice. I'm glad you didn't think I was your brother, or somebody selling encyclopedias." Both of us got a chuckle out of that, and rightly deserved on my part, I guess. "Look, you mentioned something the other night about maybe doing some revamping to your downstairs bathroom."

"Yes, Connie jumped in a little too soon, and she knew she cut him off from finishing his sentence. I wanted to see if another entry way could be made."

"I'm not a professional carpenter, or anything like that. What I mean to say is, I don't belong to any type of union or anything, but I have a pretty good working knowledge of masonry, plumbing, and can do a little electrical work."

"Wow! Is there anything else you have a good working knowledge of?"

Immediately after saying the sentence *that* way, I was embarrassed. Because, that sounded kind of provocative—even to me.
 I could only imagine how it sounded to a man.
Otis felt a surge of flesh stir up in him, but he refused to let *it* go there. "Well, he said; still a little shaken, I don't have any references, but I can show you some of my work."

Now, the shoe was on the other foot. Although what he said was a completely natural thing to say; when the devil's imps are lurking around your mind, he makes everything you say seem **unseemly**. Why is everything I'm trying to say coming out the wrong way? That sounded so *carnal*. He knew it was the enemy, so he said a short silent prayer. He clarified his words and his work.

"That is, if you want to come by the shop to see the renovations I did here you can, or I can show you some of the things I helped with at the church when we were doing some interior renovations there."

"Okay, I'm impressed."

"Well then, if I've won you over, shall we set up a date…? I mean, shall we set a date, and time for me to drop by?"

Otis could feel he was stumbling all over himself. He didn't know why his words were getting so twisted, and probably being taken in the wrong way.

"What day is more convenient for you, Connie asked?"

"How about this Saturday? Most Saturdays I only work half a day. The shop is opened from 9:00am 'til noon. That gives customers the chance to get in and pick up their repairs, and sometimes I close up early. That leaves me enough time to make personal deliveries." Connie started to say that sounded fine, and then she thought; *what if Edmund is still over here doing the yard?*

"I have an appointment on Saturday, and I'm not sure how long it will take. Could you possibly come over on Friday evening?"

"Sure, I close up at five o'clock. Is six o'clock okay?"

"Yeah, that sounds great."

"Okay. I'll see you this Friday at six."

"Thanks Otis, I really appreciate this. Bye."

"My pleasure. Goodbye."

———

Otis was hoping he would have gotten a chance to sit in the pew tonight at church. He wouldn't have sat right next to Connie, but somewhere close, either farther down on the pew where she say, or across the aisle. That was all interrupted by a phone call. He wasn't assigned to be the armor bearer on Wednesday nights in September. The person assigned had caught a bad summer cold, and Otis was asked to fill in for him. At first he was disappointed, but then he realized that he would be at a better vantage point for seeing Connie. He had to pull himself together. He was helped by a *'Holy Ghost'* knock up beside the head. He wasn't supposed to be going to Bible study to focus his attention on a woman. He was supposed to be going to Bible study to pay attention to the Word, and the new assignment given him that tonight.

Before Otis left the house, he made grave promises to himself to concentrate on his assignment for the evening. However, from his position on the pulpit, it was challenging not to pay attention to the beautiful presence of Constance Black sitting in the audience.

Some late comers straggled in the sanctuary and took vacant seats near the back. But one person came and sat in the pew behind Connie, and the open seat directly in back of her. She was always taught by her parents that it was rude, and disrespectful to turn your head and look back at people when you were sitting in church. She didn't remember why; something to do with turning your back on the *Word*, or something to do with *Lot's* wife turning into a pillar of salt when she looked back.

The older generation said a lot of things that were probably wives tales. Nonetheless, those things taught you good church manners. So she didn't look back. But, what she did notice was the look on Otis's face when the person sat directly in back of her.

A few seconds later, a voice behind me said in a whisper; "Hey baby, I took you up on your invitation." It was Marcus Yancey. My eyes opened wider, but I kept looking straight ahead of me. I didn't dare move. It's easy to forgive a person if you never have to deal with them again, but it's another thing when they show up as a constant reminder of the hurtful insults you experienced at their expense.

I didn't respond to his greeting. I just closed my eyes and began to pray. A few minutes later I felt his breath on the back of my neck when he leaned forward and said something else. I was concentrating so hard on praying for forgiveness, I didn't hear what he said.

When Bible study ended, the congregation got up row by row to put their offerings in the basket up front. I had an offering, but I remained seated. I didn't want to move. I didn't want Marcus to look at my body as I was walking. I knew he would stare indecently, and entertain inappropriate thoughts.

Otis could take in everything from where he was seated on the pulpit. And, if he was right about what was seeing, it looked like Connie was being agitated. Pastor Thornton gave the benediction, and Otis saw Marcus stand and move in on Connie before she could come out from the pew. He couldn't hear what he was saying to her, but whatever it was, if it was Marcus, Otis knew it was out of order. He asked Pastor Thornton if he was needed anymore. He told him no, and thank him for filling in tonight.

Otis grabbed his Bible, and took a couple of deep breaths. He said to himself, *the church may be public domain, but Connie Webster isn't!* He realized he didn't have the right to interfere with her personal affairs, but as an ordained deacon in the church, and a man of God, he *sure enough* had the authority to… and he was going to do just that!

Marcus was saying something to the effect that this church had some *fine* looking women in it. He was saying maybe he ought to join. My eyes began to look around the sanctuary searching for something, or someone to rescue me from this dreadful person.

Just as I was coming out of the pew, forcing myself passed Marcus, Otis came up to stand beside me. For some reason, I felt a sense of relief–a sense of protection. Otis greeted Marcus. Then without permission, or any warning he fished for my arm, found my hand, and locked his over mine. He was still looking at Marcus the whole time, and with his eyes fixed on him, he said: "Hey, what's going on here?"

Marcus' eyes went down to our interlocked hands, and then he looked back at Otis. "Hey *Bro*, so that's the way it 'Tis. I can *dig* it."

My knees began to wobble. Otis must have felt the nervousness in my hand, and he gave it a gentle squeeze as if to say—everything's going to be all right, and he never broke his eye contact with Marcus.

"It is good to see you out tonight Marcus." Otis was trying to put what he had to say to Marcus in a delicate way. "I hope you are sincere about wanting to get church back in your life, because if you're looking for a nice young lady to talk to, this is the right place to be. But, I can tell you this about most of the '*Sistahs*' in here. If you haven't walked that way first, (he nodded his head toward the altar) there is no use in trying to run a line by them up in here." Marcus tried to stiffen up to Otis. "What you' trying to say *Bro*?"

"What I'm *saying* is by this time in life, most of these ladies in here have reached their mid-thirties just like us. They've been *there*, and done *that*. *Now*, they're looking for someone who is as strong in the Lord as they are."

"Man, you all *holy* and stuff. I didn't come up in here for all *'dat*. I just wanted to check things out." That's when Otis jumped into the dialect that Marcus could understand.

"Well *my* man, you know what we used to *say* back in the *day*. If you want to check things out, go to the grocery *store*. This is real life up in here Bro. Ain't nobody playing high school games. Don't get me wrong. If you really want to turn your life around, then this is the place to do it."

Otis took one step forward, and Marcus started backing up as he moved. "Look man, I *git* it, I *git* it. That's your *woman*, and she's off the market. Stay cool, and I'll be digging you all later." He raised his hands in the air facing them toward Otis. After that, he did a quick turn on and left through the exit door. Otis and I were still holding hands, but I didn't pull away. He turned to look at me, and asked if I was all right. I said yes, and thanked him for coming to my rescue. He said he would walk me to my car just in case Marcus was still lurking around outside. He looked down at our hands, and asked me if it was okay for him to continue holding my hand. *This time*, I gave his hand a gentle squeeze, and we walked from the sanctuary to the parking lot still holding hands.

Chapter 25

On the drive home, Connie had second thoughts. Should she have let Otis hold her hand all the way to her car? She knew she wanted him to, but should she have? She was reminded of the awkward position she was in at that time. It would have been silly for her to say; *"no, you can't continue to hold my hand"* when he had been holding it all along. What did that mean to him? When a guy asks to hold a girl's hand, I know that means he likes her, but does he get the notion that she is *his girl?* When Marcus saw that our hands locked around each other's, that was certainly the idea he got. Was that a guy thing that was an unspoken code, or some sort of sign that was understood in the male arena of romance?

Connie wrestled with those thoughts for the remainder of the evening. The more she thought, the more another thoughts came into her mind. *By letting him hold my hand, did he think I was in agreement with whatever he was thinking?* In the midst of all the pondering, she was reminded that Otis was coming by on Friday. "Oh my God! Will he assume that I'm his girl?"

Otis could have kicked himself twice over. "You idiot!" he told himself. You may have ruined everything. You moved too fast. Why didn't you let her hand go right after Marcus turned to leave? But, *No you got caught up in your own bluff.* Sure. It worked in making Marcus think you and Connie were a couple, but you kept holding on to her as if you believed it yourself.

"All right Lord, what am I supposed to do now? I don't want to scare her off. But, I heard you say "*she was my wife.*" Otis was half praying and halfway having a conversation with the Lord at the same time.

Sometimes you want the Holy Spirit to answer you, and sometimes you don't. Otis had experienced the voice of God many times in his spirit-man, and he could attest that the Holy Spirit had a sense of humor, because this time he thought he heard Him chide in: *Yes, she is going to be your wife. But, I didn't mean two days after your first date!* Otis had to laugh out loud. He knew that was indeed the Lord!

He also could read between the lines. He had pushed forward a little too quickly, and some form of apology was in order.

———

Connie jumped when the telephone blasted into her silent musing. She looked at the clock on the nightstand. It was only 9:15pm. She wondered who could be calling her at that hour. She didn't want to answer, not knowing whom to expect, but she girded up her loins and answered anyway. Thank goodness, it was Levee. She, in a playful sisterly manner let Connie know she was getting ready to come over and speak to her after Bible study this evening, but she didn't have a ticket. There seemed to be a show going on, and she was afraid she would have to wait in line.

Connie knew she owed her an explanation, so she went into some of what was happening, however not telling everything. She let her sister know that this was her third encounter with Marcus, and it looked like he wasn't accepting a polite *'not interested'*. Olivia said she couldn't take long on the phone, but she wanted her sister to know that she and the *Deacon* looked pretty friendly going out the door together. Connie heard her emphasis on Deacon. They say good night, and said they will call each other before the week was out.

It wasn't quite nine thirty, so Connie thought she would sit out on the porch swing for about half an hour to think. She kicked off her sandals, and slipped her feet into her slippers. The ring of the telephone caught her just before she had a chance to get to the bedroom door. She looked at the clock. It had only been two minutes sense she hung up from Levee, so she knew her sister had forgotten to say something to her.

"Hello Levee, wha-cha forget?"

There was a slight pause, and then the gentle baritone voice of Deacon Otis Delaney came through the receiver. "Good evening. I don't mind you getting it wrong when I call. However, I draw the line at being called being girl names."

"Oh, Otis I'm so sorry. I thought …"

"I know. You thought I was your sister." "Sorry Connie said, you see she just hung up, and I thought she was calling back for something else."

"I didn't mean to cut you off. I know it's getting late, but I just wanted to call and apologize."

"Apologize? For what? I don't understand."

"For forcing you to make an uncomfortable decision in a situation where I was supposed to be helping you, and with all due respect, I'm afraid I let my personal feelings get in the way. Well, what I'm trying to say is, I know I overstepped my bounds by continuing to hold your hand."

"Thank you Otis, but there's really no need to apologize. Remember, you asked me, and I said 'yes'. But, apology accepted."

Connie was trying to hold the telephone to her ear and at the same time stretched the cord to reach to the Queen Ann easy chair. It didn't work. The base dropped from her hand and the receiver flung from her ear and hit the bed post. Connie fell to her knees scrambling and, crawled across the floor chasing the recoiling telephone cord. "Oh shoot! Darn it!"

She finally retrieved the phone and said in a more relaxed, sweet lady-like voice.

"Hello, are you still there?"

"Too late, Otis said, I heard you. What happened?" He was laughing. "Whoops! Sorry 'bout that, Connie said."

"That's alright he said, at least now I know you don't *Cuss,* or *Swear,* and…and, it let me know I'm worth chasing after."

Connie drew in a deep breath, as if to say, *I didn't say all that*! Otis said again that he didn't want to keep me, and asked if anything had changed concerning Friday night. I said no. But, I wanted to say '*yes*', my heart! He said goodbye he would see me on Friday evening.

I put the phone back on the nightstand, and went out to sit on the front stoop. I leaned my back against the pillar, and smiled pleasantly. Then, talking out loud to no one in particular but myself, I said: "Just think, twenty minutes ago you were upset and unsure about the intentions of Otis Delaney, and now you're *in love* all over again.

———

Otis grabbed a cold soda from the fridge, and went out to sit on the front stoop. Now that school started back at the beginning of the week, most of the younger children had gone in the house, or had either gone to bed. A teenage boy and girl walked hand-in-hand past his house, and he saw another couple on the other side of the street. It caused him to think about the events of the evening, and his date with Connie on Labor Day. He smiled, and thanked God for *His* providential wisdom.

Some teenage boys had gathered on the corner

about half a block down from his house. He knew the guys were doing what guys did—look at girls. The girls were strolling up one side of the block. They crossed the street at the corner, and went down on the other side. Of course, the whole object of the stroll was to get a response out of the boys. Every now and then you'd hear a loud whistle, or a "Hey baby, you sure look good" out of one of the boys. The girls would tee-hee, and pretend to act like they were ignoring the attention.

Otis shook his head in amusement. He remembered when he was one of those teenage boys back in the 50s. He loitered on the corner with some of his friends too. They boys were checking the girls out while their so called 'singing group' was trying to harmonize to some of the latest doo-wop songs. They sang "*You Belong to Me*" by the Orioles, and "Why Do Fools Fall in Love", by Frankie Lyman & the Teenagers.

Except back then, there weren't many popular songs that *black* groups sang. Most of the songs were *Ballots*, but those were the types of songs you sang if you wanted to get on the *Hit Parade*.

Otis remembered when all of the group they hung around with gathered over to the Webster's house to watch their TV when Frankie Lyman and The Teenagers came on the Frankie Laine show. "Man"! Otis said out loud. "We were so excited. That was one of the greatest moments we had ever experienced."

He came out of his reminiscing when he heard one of the parents bellow to their son from across the street that it was time to come in. The boy happened to be one of the teenagers standing with his friends on the corner.

His buddies begin to tease and razz him. They were mimicking his mother's voice; "*hey Junior, it's time to come in.*"

Otis didn't mean to laugh, but it was kind of funny. The thing about it was, the group started breaking up after that. It's probably because they knew it was close to their curfew time, and they didn't want their Mamas calling their names out the front door.

Chapter 26

Edmund's schedule was going to be sort of tight on Saturday, so he was thinking he might go by Connie's on Friday anyway. Originally she had called to ask him to come over on Saturday because she had an appointment on Friday evening. It wasn't a problem at first because he was available either day. But, after her phone call on Tuesday, some things had changed. Because people knew he and his business partner had a pickup truck, they often called on him to help them move.

Raymond was one of their regular customers. He was a frugal person, and liked to save money. He had recently received one of those *"Uncle Sam wants you"* letters, and decided to answer the *Call*. After college he moved out of his folk's house, and got an apartment of his own. He was doing pretty well for a twenty-four year old. However, he knew that when he went into the service, he would not be able to afford to keep up his apartment.

Raymond was going to store most of his things in his dad's garage, and moved back in with his dad when he returned. He said he wasn't sure what happened between his folks, but about a year or so after he moved out of his parent's house, and his sister went off to college; the next thing he knew his parents got a divorce.

Edmund didn't want to pass up the opportunity to earn a little extra income. Aside from that, he didn't know how long the move would take, given Raymond's dad lived way out near Grayson. *The best thing to do*, he thought, *is to get out to Connie's on Friday after we close up the Flea Market. It won't matter if she's not home. When she comes back from her appointment, the yard will be finished.*

Connie cleaned house all day on Thursday. She swept, dusted, gave the bathroom and extra good cleaning, she mopped and waxed the kitchen floor. She paid particular attention to her bedroom. Before she knew it the morning and afternoon had slipped away. She got a phone call from the pastor's wife welcoming her to the congregation, and thanked her for attending Bible study on Wednesday night.

Oh my goodness! The pastor and his wife were still in the sanctuary when Otis and I walked out together. I hope they didn't see us holding hands.

In her head, she fussed at herself. "Stop it!" Stop it!" *You have to stop being embarrassed and full of fear every time you think someone has seen you talking to a man. You let pride get in your way the first time around with Otis, and you married a man you thought could take his place. Now, God has put Otis back in your life, and you don't want to blow this second chance.* After hearing what she heard, Connie wasn't sure if it was her mind was the one talking, or if it was the Holy Spirit.

The next morning Connie woke from a very pleasant dream. Finally, it was Friday! She knew before her own mind started dictating things to her, the first thing on the agenda should be her devotional time and prayer. She could hear her parents saying, *'Put God first, and He will direct the rest of your day.'*

After she prayed, Connie was right in the middle of reading some Bible passages when her mind strayed to what else she could do to fill her day. Instantly she heard in her spirit, *'cook dinner for Otis'*. She knew that must have been the Lord, because here lately, she wasn't one to prepare a full dinner even for herself. She selected a few more passages to read, and closed her Bible. That makes sense she thought. Otis will probably be coming over here straight from work. Connie had no idea what to prepare. She started to call Levee, and on her way to the telephone the answer came into her head. She made a U-turn, and went to the kitchen 'catch all' drawer to get her grandmother's recipe cards.

The shop stayed busy most of the morning, and Otis was glad. He finished repairing the smaller jobs yesterday, things like replacing a burned-out radio tube, frayed wires on extension cords, and replacing missing knobs on radio and TV sets. Earlier in the week he worked on things like aligning the convergence and fixing the brightness problem on a customer's television. He even completed the repairs on a color TV he had in the shop for over two weeks. That was because he ran into a few problems, and told the customer he had to send away for the schematic of the chaise in order to figure out how to finish repairing his TV. Otis told him when that came in on Tuesday, he had no problem with the repairs.

One of the deacons from the church came in to pick up a repaired radio for his mother. The two men chatted for a while, and then Otis asked him if he wouldn't mind staying at the shop for a few minutes while he ran down to the corner to pick up a pizza. Otis knew he wouldn't have time to grab anything for dinner before going over to Connie's place. So, he called the pizzeria for a pickup order. It was already past two o'clock, and he had not eaten lunch.

Otis hurried back, and thanked Charles for staying at the shop. He told him how much he appreciated the favor, because he didn't want to close the shop just to go pick up a burger and onion rings.

Usually he would have bought along something for lunch, but this morning when he got up he was a little sidetracked... thinking about Connie.

Otis was relieved that he didn't have any deliveries to make. He still closed the shop a half hour earlier than his usual Friday hours. He went straight home to shower and shave. Getting dressed he thought about his feelings for Connie. He never really had falling *out* of love with her.

His conscience bothered him about that. He tried to put all the love he had into his previous marriage, but there was always a corner of his heart that was never released his first love.

Did his wife sense that? Did she feel it in their closeness? Heck, he thought, Belinda was the one who pushed herself into my life. Even when I told her repeatedly that I still was in love with someone else. She told me she understood, and assured me that the love she had for me would make me forget all about my past love, and we would have a good marriage as husband and wife.

———————

Connie was satisfied with what she planned to prepare for dinner. The index cards were very helpful, yet she still decided to give Olivia a call. She was so used to doing everything on her own when she lived in Nashville. Now that she was back home, she needed to be more involved with family anyway.

Levee was the cook in the family, and had some pointers for me about the meal I had come up with. Of course I had to tell her why I wanted to cook such a complete dinner tonight. I didn't want the meal to be something fancy, just a nice home cooked meal. She told me what I might want to get from the store. I went to Winn Dixie, and picked up a whole chicken, and some fresh snap beans. I had can beans in the cupboard, but Levee suggested using fresh beans. She wanted me to keep her informed on everything that was happening. I promised her I would, and reminded her that *Mums* the word until further notice.

Connie decided to freshen up before Otis arrived. She didn't want to use the downstairs bathroom, so she went upstairs. She removed her headscarf, and took off her housecoat. She turned the shower on, and placed her change of clothes on the vanity chair.

Edmund pulled the truck into his sister's drive way. He went to the back of the truck to unload the lawnmower. He had just put the gasoline in the mower, and was about to rev up the motor when Mrs. Miller came by. She spoke to Edmund, but instead of her continuing on down to street, she turned into the driveway. He could tell she wanted to talk, or to spread gossip, and he didn't have time for either one.

"Hello, there Eddie."

"Hello Mrs. Miller. How are you today?"

"Oh, I'm doing fine sonny. How's your sister?"

"She's doing okay, but I don't think she's home right now. She had an appointment this evening."

"I'm surprised you came over to cut the grass, I would think that Deacon Delaney would be cutting it for her by now."

"O yeah, why is that?"

"Well, you know, on account of the way they've become so friendly here lately. He's been over here a couple times this week. And I'd be surprised if he wasn't going to pay her a visit tonight." She let out a little tee-hee.

Edmund knew Mrs. Miller meant well, but she could stretch the truth at times. She had been known to mix up the gossip she heard. Some tales were pretty much on point–however the others you had to take with a grain of salt. Edmund didn't want to cut her off, but he did have to get the yard cut and then get the truck back to be cleaned for its moving job tomorrow.

Connie stepped from the shower, and grabbed the bath towel from the hook on the wall. She heard the distant drone of a lawnmower. *Hum,* she thought, one of the neighbors must be getting their yard cut. She put on her makeup and dressed before coming down to her room. *That's funny,* she thought. Now the noise sounds even closer almost as if it's right outside of my house. She stopped in her tracks, and went around the bed to peek through the curtain at the back window. Connie's heart flew up to her mouth, and she felt a little nauseous. Oh my God! What am I going to do? Otis will be here any minute now.

She ran across the hall, opened the door that led into the garage, and whipped the side door open that led to the backyard. Edmund's back was turned to her as he walked towards the trees that lined the perimeter. Connie didn't want to walk across the yard after him, because freshly cut grass would stick to her shoes, and flying dust would settle on her hair and clean clothes. She had to wait until he turned around to come back towards the house.

Edmund was singing almost as loud as the lawnmower was humming; *"Poison I-vaaa-ay, poison i-vaaa-ay, late at night while you're sleeping poison ivy comes a creeping around-ound-ound-ound."* He looked up to see Connie waving both of her arms back and forth in the air. "What in the world is she doing home? I thought she was gone for an appointment."

He turned the mower off, and trotted the short distance across the yard to where his sister was standing. She seemed a little frustrated. So he explained what happened with his schedule, and why he had to cut the grass now. But that didn't seem to be the problem. So, he asked her what was going on, and what difference did it make that he was cutting the grass now.

Connie had to come clean and told him what was going on. She explained that Deacon Delaney was coming over this evening, but she quickly added that it was only to see if it was possible to make a second entry way for the downstairs bathroom.
"Wow! He thought smiling to himself. *I'll never doubt Mrs. Miller's gossip again!"*
Connie apologized to her brother, saying things just began to escalate and she still wasn't sure what it would be. Edmund said he was happy for her, and tried to give his sister a brotherly hug. Connie jumped away pushing him back and said, "Don't you dare hug me with your dusty, sweaty self." Edmund told her he was almost finished, and he'd probably be gone before the *"Deek"* got there.

 # Honey Glazed Carrots

1lb. bag/or box frozen baby carrots
[Syrup mixture]
¼ cup honey
¼ cup brown sugar
¼ cup water
2 tablespoons butter
(Dash) cinnamon

Directions: Put carrots in boiling water, cover. Cook until done, but still slightly firm. [In separate sauce pan] Combine honey, water, and brown sugar. Bring mixture to a boil. Reduce heat, and cook until mixture thickens into a syrup—about 15 min. Stir occasionally. Drain carrots and stir in butter. Add in Honey mixture, and cook for another 5 minutes. Serve

Chapter 27

Otis pulled up to Connie's house and saw a pickup truck parked in the driveway. The truck looked familiar to him, but he couldn't be sure of whom it belong to. The first thought that popped into his mind was that Connie must have invited someone else to come over so she wouldn't be alone in the house with him. *No, that can't be it*, he told himself, because I've been over here before. He guessed he could have parked his car on the street, but he wasn't comfortable with that.

The pickup truck was parked right in the middle of the driveway making it hard for another vehicle to park on either side of it. He pulled his car in the driveway, maneuvered close to the truck on the left side, and parked. He could tell his tires were on the lawn. Just then he heard the sound of a lawnmower. Someone must be cutting Connie's grass. "That's it! Otis said out loud, I knew I'd seen that truck somewhere before. It belongs to her brother Edmund."

The hum of the mower stopped, and Otis got out of his car. Edmund emerged from around the side of the house. He was pushing a lawnmower, and stopped when he saw a man standing beside his truck in the driveway. He took off his baseball cap and wiped his brow with the back of his forearm. Moving a little closer, and coming up on the other side of his truck he noticed who the man was. Edmund met Deacon Delaney coming around to the back of the truck, and he wiped his hand on his jeans, extending toward Otis.

"Hi *'Deek'*, I was trying to move out of here before Connie's company showed up."
"Hey! Eddie. No need for that '*Brother*'."

"Well, you know how it 'Tis'. Sisters don't want little brothers hanging around when they're expecting company. I was 'spose to do this tomorrow, but I've gotta help somebody move."

"I'm just going to take a quick look around in the bathroom to see if Connie's idea of a second entryway is going to work out. No need to run off. It probably won't take me more than a few minutes."

Edmund lifted the mower onto the back of the truck, and Otis helped him to stabilize it. Then he set the gasoline can down into a wooden crate. Edmund was standing facing the house, and his eyes fell on Connie who was standing at the Parlor window. She was waving her hand motioning for him to go.

Otis was standing with his back towards the house, and was telling him that he could move the car around to the garage, or even back it out onto the street. Edmund glanced slightly toward the window again, and this time Connie was gliding her index finger across her throat in a long slicing motion. Edmund's eyes bucked, and he got the message. He turned to Otis and said, "Nah man that's okay *Deek*, I really gotta go. I have to get the lawnmower back to the shop, and then washed the truck down for tomorrow."

He hopped in the truck and turned on the key. He saw Connie step back from the window, and the curtain draped back into place.

As soon as Otis came up on the porch Connie opened the door. He smelled the aroma of fried chicken. He didn't intend for his eyes to wander towards the kitchen, but they did.

"Come on in Connie said, following the movement of his eyes. I thought maybe you would be heading over here right after work, so I figured the least I could do was to cook us a little something for dinner."

"Gee, Thanks. But you didn't have to go through all that trouble. I could've picked something up on the way home."

Otis knew that picking up fast food on the way home was nothing to look forward to over and above a home cooked meal, and that was what he hoping was for—a reason to extend his visit with Connie. "Oh, it wasn't any trouble at all. I had to eat dinner anyway." Connie knew good and well she had slaved most of the day cooking that meal, but when she answered the door she made sure she was looking fresh as a newly picked Daisy.

Otis bought in an extending measuring tape, a sketchpad, and a couple of pencils. Connie led him down the hallway to her bedroom. Otis had been over to the Webster's house many times when he and Connie were dating and even afterwards, but he had never ventured back this far. He felt a little strange knowing that he was about to go into Connie's bedroom.

In anticipation of his coming, Connie removed the clothes that were hanging on the right side of her closet, and laid them on the bed. It opened the closet up little more so one wouldn't feel so close in. It also made the bed look less inviting. Connie was just being honest with herself. *Let's face it,* she thought, *Flesh is flesh. Nothing good can come of tempting yourself in an area where you may already feel you are becoming weak.* She also grabbed the suitcase, and a box that held her winter boots, and put them on the bed too.

Otis commented on how nicely the room was decorated. It was large and spacious. Connie told him her mother was responsible for most of that decorating, all she did was to switch out the comforter and pillow shams when she moved in. A melancholy moment engulfed her, and she shook it off.

Connie knew that Otis was a very detailed person, and a bit of a perfectionist. He went into the walk-in closet, and before she left the room, Connie tried to think of a delicate way to tell him not to be too long measuring and drawing, because dinner was ready, and waiting. How could she suggest that without sounding *too* bossy or come off as wife-ish'?

Before she could move, Otis stuck his head around the closet opening and said, "Hey Constance, I think I'm just going to take a few measurements, and then go to my car to get my Polaroid. I'll take some pictures of the closet and the bathroom, that way you won't have to hold dinner for me. By the way, it smells *mighty* good!"

Connie left the room, and strutted down the hallway beaming with pride. But she knew she didn't do it all by herself, she had her grandmother and Levee to thank too. She set the table while Otis was busy gathering measurements and snapping pictures. She didn't hear Otis when he came into the kitchen, and was caught off guard when he said, "Hey Connie." When she turned around, he took her picture. She was standing at the stove dipping the string beans into a glass serving bowl, and was still wearing her apron.

"Otis! She squealed, that wasn't fair. I wasn't ready to have my picture taken. Look at me. I still have my apron on, and I look like an *old* housewife, or… *something.*"
"So, what's wrong with that? That something looks pretty good to me."

He lowered the camera from his face, and for a brief moment their eyes met in silence. Otis cleared his throat, and excused himself to go put his things back in the car. Outside, he looked up to see Mrs. Miller passing by the house. He waved his hand and gave her a "Good evening" greeting, and she returned the gesture. He said to himself, *this is the third time I've visited Connie, but this is the first time I can remember seeing Sister Miller.*

Connie usually prayed over her meal before eating, but since a man was present at her dinner table, she asked him to say the grace. That's one of the things she learned from her mother. No matter how far up the spiritual ladder a woman may be, when a gentleman is at the table (especially a man of God) you should always give him the honor of saying the blessing.

Otis complemented Connie on the delicious food several times and said it reminded him of her mother's cooking. That statement caused an unexpected silence from both of them. Otis apologized, and asked if she was all right. Connie said she was okay. They shared great conversation during the meal, and Otis mentioned that he couldn't remember if he had ever tasted any of her cooking when they were dating. Connie said she was sure he hadn't, because she didn't cook that much when she was a teenager.

The way Otis was enjoying the food Connie figured he must have been starving for a home cooked meal. He ate three pieces of fried chicken, two helpings of homemade mashed potatoes, a little more of the string beans, and three buttermilk biscuits with butter and honey. Otis said the last time he had eaten that hearty was at the church picnic. But before then, he believed the last home-cooked meal he had was over to Pastor Thornton's house.

He said the pastor and his wife invited him often, but he only took them up on the offer once or twice. He didn't want to become a pest. And, besides that, he said he was becoming a pretty fair bachelor cook… Connie wasn't sure what that meant.

Otis insisted on helping Connie clear the table and to wash the dishes. She was okay with them clearing the table together and putting away the food, but when it came to standing side-by-side with a man putting your hands in warm, sudsy dishwater together—she opted out. She had been married once, and she knew how sensual warm sudsy water could be. Otis felt like he really wanted to stay and watch TV when Connie offered, but he knew the whole evening had already surpassed his expectations. He was really being drawn to Connie, and to sit with her on the sofa would be stretching his ability to resist the temptation that was welling up in him all evening long.

Chapter 28

Levee couldn't wait for her sister to call her, so she called Connie instead. She asked her to come over for breakfast. As a matter of fact, she demanded Connie come to breakfast. Of course, she said it in a loving, sisterly sort of way. Olivia told her she had no excuse. Her house was clean, her grass was cut, and it had been a couple of weeks since her last visit. Connie gave in. She knew Olivia was right. What the heck, she needed somebody to confide in anyway. It might as well be someone she trusted, and loved.

Levee wanted to hear everything. Earl Junior had eaten breakfast, and was now in the living room sitting in front of the TV. It was Saturday morning, and he was watching all of his favorite cartoon shows. From the kitchen they were able to keep an eye on him, but Levee assured Connie that he would be glued to the set for the next two hours.

Connie shared last evening's events with her sister, even the part about Edmund unexpectedly showing up. Connie said she wasn't really upset with him. She was just glad he didn't try to invite himself to dinner. Both of them laughed knowing their brother all too well. Connie admitted that she was very much drawn to Otis, but things were going *too* fast too soon. She said she wanted to separate the old high school feelings she had for him, from what she thought she was feeling for him now. She didn't want to get the two feelings mixed up.

Olivia understood her sister's concerned, and offered her another thought. She said she believed her feelings for Otis were genuine. But, maybe they seemed to stir up so quickly because they were never meant to be interrupted. She said, "Suppose in some kind of *mystical*, *magical* sort of way you two were meant to be husband and wife a long time ago. You know, true love separated… and now God is bridging the path that tore y'all part."

I had forgotten how dramatic Levee could be. She is the creative one in the family, but what she said (without the drama) made sense. We talked some more, sharing about old times. Before I left, I told her I planned on being at church a little earlier because I wanted to join a Sunday school class. Levee suggested the Adult Sunday school class. It met in the sanctuary from 9:30 a.m. to 10:30 a.m. I thanked her again for everything, and said give my nephew a big hug for me. I didn't dare try to kiss him again.

On the drive home I asked myself questions like: How do you know if you really love somebody? When does *like* turned into *love*? Do you end up just being in love, or was there a point where you could say you *fell* in love? I stopped by the drugstore and purchase some pantyhose and fingernail polish remover. I was still thinking about the 'love' thing when I got home. I believed Mom and Pop really loved each other. I only wished I could ask her how she knew Pop was the *one*. Does love happen before you marry, or do you grow in love after you marry?

If Levee was the creative one in the family, then I was the romantic. Even when I agreed to marry Anthony, I knew I didn't feel the same way about him that I did about Otis.

I went over to the Hi-fi and found the Nat King Cole album. I just had to hear him sing, *"When I Fall in Love"*. His mellow, smooth voice filled the room and impacted my heart. That's what I want. I want love to be like those words.

> *When I fall in love, it will be forever, or I'll never fall in love… When I give my heart, it would be completely, or I'll never give my heart…*

Connie grabbed one of the throw pillows next to her, held it to her bosom, and let the tears flow.

Otis closed the repair shop at noon. One of the things he'd been considering was to change his Saturday store hours. He didn't like getting up, and getting out that early on Saturday mornings, and it appeared that his regular Saturday customers didn't favor it much either. When they did come in, it was usually closer to eleven o'clock. That meant that most of the early morning he was in the shop by himself. It did allow him to tinker around with repairs that were scheduled to be ready for the next week, but it put him in a bind when everyone seemed to come the last hour before closing to pick up their repairs.

Maybe, he thought, *if I change the nine to twelve store hours to 10 a.m. to 2 p.m. it would be better for business. Who knows? I might even have a date on a Friday evening, and not want to get up so early to open the store by nine o'clock in the morning.*

Otis swung by the barbershop to get his hair trimmed. There was the usual manly banter and gossip going on. If people thought only women gossiped, they ought to spend an hour in a barbershop. Otis was glad he wasn't the bunt of any of the razzing going on this week. But, he was pretty sure that when he and Constance Weber-Black showed up somewhere for their first public date he'd probably have to change barbershops.

Otis didn't want to go right home. Since it was almost two in the afternoon, he thought he could catch a matinee at the movies. It sounded like a good idea at first, but a second thought hit him. It was Saturday afternoon. The theaters would be filled with kids, and some of their parents. Mainly the kids will be there with their older brothers or sisters, (who by the way) were not trying to be seen sitting with their younger siblings. They wanted to sit as far away from them as they possibly could just in case a cute boy, or girl was looking their way.

If he went later on in the evening he could see "The French Connection", "Dirty Harry, or the new James Bond movie, "Diamonds Are Forever". But then again, who wanted to sit alone at the movies? It's hopeless he thought. Why is it that some places I used to go along didn't bother me, but now that Connie's back in my life, if I go by myself my aloneness seems to magnify?

Otis decided to go home, and see if he could draw up any ideas to reconstruct Connie's bathroom.

———

Connie came out of her stupor, and was tempted to call Otis. First, she had to come up with a good enough to reason call him. *She avoided the word* excuse. I'll call him to see how the sketches are coming along for the bathroom. *No,* she thought, *I'll call him to say he didn't show me the photo he took of me last night, and if could he bring it to church with him tomorrow.* Everything Connie thought of sounded *lame* and weak, because the truth of the matter was she was putting out a *'chase',* and she didn't know why. Otis was already interested in her, so why was she falling into a desperate mood? She knew it was just because she wanted to hear *his* voice.

She resolved her feelings in a short request, asking the Lord to help her to wait until tomorrow. She went to her bedroom and opened the closet door. She began to look over her wardrobe to find something nice to wear for church. *Let me see,* she thought. *It's mid-September. I don't need to wear anything white, and I'm cutting back on the pastels.* When she was satisfied with what she wanted to wear for Sunday, Connie went to the kitchen to warm up leftovers from last evening's meal. She took her dinner plate and her drink to the living room, and searched through the TV Guide.

Otis picked up his sketchpad, pencil, a twelve-inch ruler, and sat at the kitchen table. He made a few sketches, and still couldn't get a good idea of what would work. He went to the bedroom to get the Polaroid pictures from off the dresser. He came back to the table and spread them out one by one. He stopped when he got to the picture of Connie. He held it up in his hand and smiled. Otis looked at her photo for several minutes recapturing the whole evening. He felt a strong urge to give Connie a call, but what would he say to her. He had already thanked her for the dinner. He couldn't say he had finished sketches, because he had not completed even one.

Otis arrived at church about fifteen minutes before Sunday school started. He knew Pastor Thornton would be in his office, and he wanted to ask his advice about something. Ordinarily he wouldn't have bothered the pastor with any personal problems on a Sunday morning especially if he had to preach the sermon for that day. But, this was 'Men's Day', and they had a guest speaker coming in. Otis was to be the armor bearer for the visiting preacher. He went to the pastor's office, and tapped on the door.

He briefly shared with Pastor Thornton his recent involvement with Connie, and wanted to know if he should give her more time before he approached her about a deeper relationship. Pastor Thornton said from what he *saw* on Wednesday night, it looked like I had already indicated that. I explained to him what that situation was all about. He said that may have been my intention, but in doing what I did, I had already placed myself in the role of wanting a deeper relationship. I was her friend, her protector, and now, because of doing the work on the bathroom I was even becoming her helper. "What more is there left to do but to see if you and she feel the same way about each other–that is in a romantic way of course? And, if she says she does then, young man I would follow my heart."

The Sunday school class was already in progress when Otis entered the sanctuary. He was pleasantly surprised when his eyes fell on Constance Weber. Otis was sure if a review quiz had been given after the lesson was over, that neither he, nor Connie would have been able to pass the test. When he looked up, she was looking at him, and when she looked up he was looking at her. They could only hope that they weren't as conspicuous to anyone else as they felt to themselves.

All of the Sunday school classes met in the sanctuary for a collective review of their individual lessons. After that ended there was a fifteen minute break before the morning service started. Otis knew he had to get back to the pastor's office to be on duty, so he swiftly eased over to where Connie was standing. Almost with one long, rushing breath he said: "I don't know how you feel about this, but I'm sure I'm in love with you and I hope you feel the same way about me. So if you say yes, I'd like to affirm–that is with your permission…that we officially become a couple."

Connie looked into Otis' eyes and said, "Yes, you may *so* affirm." He knew she was making light of the language he used, but he didn't mind.

We are a couple! Otis leaned towards her and gave her a quick '*Holy-Hug*', and whispered "Thank you" in her ear. He left the sanctuary to be on post at the pastor's office, and could only hope that when he left he was walking normal, because inside his heart he was doing *loop-de-loops*. Woo-hoo!

Chapter 29

Levee and her family came in and found some space on the pew where I was sitting. She sat next to me, placing Earl Jr. between her and her husband. The congregation stood to sing the morning hymn "My Hope is built on Nothing Less." Levee leaned closer to me and asked, "How did you enjoy Sunday school?" I turned my head slightly to the left to give her my answer, and noticed she had a smirk on her face and one eyebrow was raised. I held my hymnbook up higher to cover the bottom part of my face. "Wait a minute, I whispered, you *knew* that Otis came to that Sunday school class didn't you?"

The congregation was beginning the third stanza of the hymn, and Libby looking straight ahead sang out with a clear, raised voice: *"His oath, His covenant, His blood; Support me in whelming flood; When all around my soul gives away, He then is all my Hope and stay."*

I could see she was getting some approving smiles and nods of the head from a few of the elderly members who loved to hear young adults enjoying the old hymns of the church. I whispered out of the corner of my mouth. "Thanks little Sis.", and then I joined in on the chorus.

"On Christ the solid Rock I stand; all other ground is sinking sand, all other ground is sinking sand."

229

After the guest speaker finished his message, the offering plate was being passed around. I guess that Levee must have noticed more than the usual eye contact between me and Otis, and asked if there was something I needed to tell her. We were sitting on the pews near the front of the sanctuary, so instead of conversing, I wrote a few words on the bottom of my bulletin, and passed it to her.

'We're officially a couple'

An unexpected gasp escaped her lips, and her husband reached over their son to see if she was all right. She patted her stomach (for the benefit of the other on-lookers), but passed my bulletin to her him. She nodded her head to the right of her indicating me, and then bowled it towards the pulpit. Earl's face lit up in a broad smile. I immediately put my index finger up to my lips, while my eyes *sent* the message saying, '*private information*'. He nodded, and sent the bulletin back down to me.

When service ended, Otis signaled to Connie to wait for him. The pastor and guest speaker greeted parishioners as they filed around to shake their hands. The kitchen committee planned a dinner gathering in the fellowship Hall in honor of Men's Day. All were invited, and during the announcements, the clerk reminded church members to wait until all guest had been served. Otis walked the two pastor's over to the fellowship Hall, and was released from his post for the day. He was on his way back to the sanctuary to meet up with Connie when someone tapped him on the arm. He looked around to see Mrs. Miller standing at his elbow. She greeted him with a big grin on her face.

"Well, it's about time!" "Excuse me?" Otis was confused. "It's about time you and Constance got back together again."

Otis was shocked. *What in the world? I don't believe it! I only ask Connie to be my lady less than two hours ago, and Sister Miller is gossiping about it already! I'm sure nobody said anything to her about it.* Then, his mind went back to Friday evening when she saw him over to Connie's house.

"Oh, he said with a little lightness in his voice. You must be referring to Friday evening when you saw me in her driveway. Please don't get the wrong idea. I was over there strictly on business. There are some repairs she needs to be done, and knowing that I know a little about plumbing and carpentry, she wanted to see if I had any suggestions before she went into great expense to repair them."

That sounded pretty good to Otis, so he thought he was off the hook. But then she said: "I 'spose it was business the other two times you came to visit her too." That caught him off guard. He had to think of something fast. "Okay, Okay, you caught me."

Then using his most cherished *son*–pleading voice he said; "I really want to get back with Connie and make it work for us this time, but I can't do it if rumors go out about us before she says yes. *Soo,* if we could keep this little secret between the two of us that will help me out a lot. You know how other ladies *are*, he said, giving her hand a light squeeze. One little thing can upset the whole milk cart, and ruin everything."

Mrs. Miller looked down at her hand, and said warmly, "You're such a nice deserving young man. I wouldn't want to say anything to ruin it for you and Constance. It almost broke my heart the first time y'all split up." Otis gave her a big hearty "Holy-hug" squeeze, and said "Thank you." She told him *'mums'* the word, and with a broad smile on her face that displayed several missing teeth, she sashayed towards the fellowship Hall. Otis saw Connie standing outside of the sanctuary doors. She had a blushing smile on her face that matched the one that was on his.

Earlier during the morning service, Otis was thinking of how nice it would be to sit next to or either across from Connie during the dinner, but with this new development he wasn't so sure. He shared with her what had just happened between him and Mrs. Miller. He said he wasn't ready to put her *'mum'* to the test this soon. Connie agreed. She admitted that Earl and her sister knew. Otis said he hadn't confirmed it with Pastor Thornton, but he was pretty sure he knew. That meant that too many eyes would be following their every move at the fellowship dinner. Otis suggested they skip the dinner in the fellowship Hall, and Connie agreed.

The original plan that Otis had in mind was to ask Connie about becoming a couple, have dinner at church, and then invite her out for a movie. Since a little glitch interrupted his original plan, he offered to take Connie out for dinner, which may work better on their behalf since most of the people they knew were still at church. He followed Connie back to her house in his car so she could leave her car there. She parked in front of the garage so it could be visible. This was the second time Connie had ridden in the car with Otis. They talked on the way, and Connie asked where they were going. Otis wasn't sure, but suggested an afternoon trip into Atlanta?

"I was thinking we could go to **The Varsity**, he said." Connie was excited about that. It had been years since she had been there. If they were lucky enough, maybe they would get the famous car hop *'Flossie Mae'*. *If not*, she thought, we could still have fun practicing up on our Varsity *Lingo*. A voice came over the intercom speaker.

"What'll ya have? What'll ya have! What'll ya have?" *Wow, we were at The Varsity!* Connie got tickled when Otis tried giving the waiter their order. He did all right, it's just that he put a little too much slang in his voice.

"Yeah, I'll have a Heavy Weight, Strings, and a Coke, and she'll have a Glorified Steak, Bag of Rags, and a Strawberry shake." We were both laughing so hard it's a good thing we wrote our order on a piece of torn paper, otherwise we would not have remember what we ordered when it came. Otis had a hot dog with extra chili, the order of French fries, and a Coke. I ordered a hamburger with mayonnaise, lettuce and tomato, potato chips, and a medium Strawberry milkshake.

Connie told Otis she was glad he chose *The Varsity* because they got to sit by themselves and talk. She said she would feel more comfortable once they got to know each other again. Otis agreed. After all, there had been a fourteen year gap since their last relationship ended during college. They had grown up, matured, and had a lot to catch up on. When the moment presented itself, Otis said they could continue to sit and talk alone if she wanted to go to the movies tonight. Connie wanted to know how they could sit alone at the movies and talk. He told her they could if they were at the Drive-In Theater.

———————

Otis dropped Connie off at her house and said he would be back around 8:00 pm. Connie wanted to relax and to refresh herself. She had been gone since early that morning. Otis said he wanted to do the same thing. Connie realized she had not been to a Drive-In movie since college. It was such a long time ago she didn't even know that they were still around. Her next thought was to call Levee.

She knew her phone probably had been ringing off the hook since right after church. Connie would give her a call this time, but she was firm on one thing, she would make it very clear to her that she was not going to be calling her to share every little thing that happened every time she went out with Otis. Both of them were grown adults and were deserving of their privacy.

Connie dialed her sister's number. Sure enough, Levee had called several times. Connie explained why she and Otis opted out of the Men's Day dinner. There were just too many eyes that would be sitting at those tables watching their every move. Even though people meant well, she thought their ability to act as if nothing had happened between she and Otis could be expecting too much of them. Connie told her they were going to the movies in the evening. She purposely didn't say the Drive-In. She knew how some people's mind worked when you said you were going to one of those.

Otis showed up at Connie's house promptly at 8:00 p.m., and she was ready. That's one of the things he remembered, and appreciated about her when they were dating. She was always ready. He said they could go to either one of the Starlight-Six Drive-In theaters. There was one on Moreland Avenue, and one on Memorial Drive. Either one would be okay; except the one on Moreland Avenue was larger. It had twin movie screens. The one on Memorial Drive was closer. They had already driven out of town once this afternoon, so they decided to go to the one on Memorial Drive.

"The first show should be letting out by the time we get there", Otis said. The families would usually load up the car with the kids and go to the earlier shows. That way it was still light out when the kids played in the mini play area, or when they went back and forth to the Concession stand. Otis was right. We inched along in the line of cars going in on one side of the dirt and gravel surface while the attendant directed the outgoing traffic through the exit across the way.

We found the spot where we wanted to park and Otis rolled the car window halfway up, and hooked the speaker box in place. He adjusted the volume control, and asked if I wanted anything to eat or drink. I told him not at the time, maybe later on. I can't remember the name of the movie that we were supposed to be watching, because we came there, and did just what we said we wanted to do: sit and talk in a public place—in private. We knew that one of the first things in a relationship is to gain each other's confidence and trust. In regards of that, we were willing to open up and share our past failures and mistakes.

Some things we already knew about each other's past, but what we didn't know was how it affected us personally, and the way it would play into our future relationship. I told Otis it was hard for me to put trust in another relationship because of what happened to me in my first marriage; that from that point on I only trusted in me. He listened. That was something that didn't happen when I was married to Anthony. He never listened! When Otis said he understood my feelings, I could hear in his voice that he really *understood*. He said he would do everything within his power, and with the help of the Lord to win over my trust in him. At one point I began to cry, and he handed me his handkerchief and reached for my free hand.

The word 'INTERMISSION' popped up on the movie screen and an animated hot dog began singing a jingle about the Concession Stand. Before Otis left to get our refreshments, I told him I didn't want us to get back together because of the grief and sadness we had shared. Otis looked at me and said, "Let me share something with you. I have been hurt over, and over again by the woman I was married to. I've been verbally abused for my faith, and had the wind knocked out of me when she told me she had gotten rid of my *seed,* not once, but twice! Yes, she aborted my children.

Yet she divorced me, and left. And do you know what got me through the anguish of those years after that? It was you. You were married and nowhere around, but I survived on the remembrance of the love I had for you. When I felt like giving up and throwing in the towel, I had to reach way down in that little corner of my heart that housed what *love* really felt like. No, no Constance. It's not out of grief, or sadness that I want to try again. It's out of love. Because, the last time I saw love…was the last time I saw you!"

I was stunned. I sat there in a stupefied trance. Otis reached for the handkerchief that was still in my hand, and wiped his own tears. Then he blew out a couple of deep breaths. I asked him if he was all right, and he said; "I am now." I scooted closer to him, and he wrapped his arm around my shoulder. We sat there in silence until the screen put up a message: **"Last call for the Concession Stand"**.

But, that didn't matter to us. We looked into each other's eyes and realized our '*hungers*' had been resolved. We sat there in silence until the movie ended.

 # **Southern Fried Chicken**

(2) 2 pound chickens – cut up
¼ cup all-purpose flour
Butter
Solid vegetable shortening
1 teaspoon salt
Ground black pepper (to taste)
Other seasonings (Optional)

Directions: Mix flour, salt and pepper in a paper/plastic bag. Put chicken pieces in bag and shake well. Using a large cast-iron skillet, melt enough butter and vegetable shortening to cover bottom up to 2 inches. Heat. Test by putting a pinch of bread in hot grease. It should bubble and brown in a couple of seconds.

Add chicken, cook slowly until bottom side browns (about 10 min). Turn chicken over, cover skillet and cook for 10-15 minutes. Turn again. Cook for another few minutes, check to see if chicken is thoroughly cooked inside. Remove from skillet and place on paper towel to drain. (Serves 6)

Chapter 30

On the drive home Connie continued to sit close to Otis, and he drove with his left hand so he could keep his right arm around her shoulder. It was about eleven o'clock when he pulled the car into her driveway. He parked close to the house. Otis got out of the car and went around to the passenger side to open the door for Connie. He felt different and proud, because now she was *his girl* again. Otis walked her up the front stoop and saw her to the door.

Suddenly and awkwardness on how to say 'good night' came over him. He was already holding her hand, so he shifted his body to stand directly in front of her. He knew he had to be careful. With the manners of a gentleman he said, "May I", and Connie nodded her head yes. He placed a light, tender kiss on the corner of her lips. Otis was about to step back when Connie found his mouth, and returned a gentle kiss on his lips. They didn't linger. It was short and sweet. Connie whispered "Good Night. I had a wonderful day", and then turned towards the door. Otis said Good night, and started to leave, but half way down the steps he turned back and said in a jokingly way, "You *do* realize that since you kissed me back, you'll have to marry me now."

He laughed, and looked up and down the street. Connie asked him what he was looking for. "You never know, he said, Sister Miller may come walking by four a mid-night stroll". "I just wanted to make sure your reputation is safe."

Otis ran down the steps and hopped into the car. He started the engine, said good night again, and Connie went into the house.

The first thing Otis did when he got to his bedroom was to hit the floor with prayer. He knelt beside his easy chair, and thanked God for this blessed day in his life. Then, he continued to pray because he may have been joking with Connie, but he knew that the lightness of her kiss really stirred something inside of him.

"Dear God, You know how men are. I am a man; and I don't mind saying that that innocent little kiss stirred me up. Some things in me have been dormant for a long time. I'm praying because I feel my flesh (and You know what I mean) coming to life. I know it's not Connie's doing, and according to 1Corinthians10:13, it's surely not Your doings. So please show me a way of escape, before I messed things up. I need some help at this moment, because my mind may be willing... But the flesh sure is weak. Amen."

Connie thanked God for releasing her from the fear of going into a new relationship. She still was concerned about the kiss she gave Otis. She didn't realize that her flesh could be that stirred from an innocent kiss on the lips. But then, she remembered she had been abstinent, and her flesh has been in a 'virgin' state for the past ten years. There was only one thing to do. She would talk to Otis about it. No use going into a relationship unless both parties agreed. She had to go downtown in the morning to drop off a few things at the Cleaners, so maybe she would stop by his shop.

Connie looked in the Yellow Pages of the phone directory, and found listed under TV and Radio Repairs Shops, the address and number for Otis's shop. She parked her car at one of the parking meters in front of the Dry Goods store. She put in a quarter and two dimes, hoping that would give her enough time to do all she needed to do. She knew the cleaners would only take a few minutes, however she wasn't sure how long she would visit with Otis.

Connie walked the half block down to the cleaners, and crossed the corner in front of the pizzeria. She took the piece of paper out of her purse and looked at the address she had written down. Connie stopped to gaze in the window of a little boutique someone had opened up. She was tempted to go in and browse around, but knew she would be only stalling for a few extra minutes before she had to face Otis. There it was just two more doors down from where she was standing—O'D's TV Supply and Repair Shop. She sucked in a deep breath, and blew it out slowly. Connie was sure she would chicken out when she saw him.

Otis was the kind of guy who didn't think about how appealing he was to the opposite sex, or at least he didn't act like it. He was slender and tall, but muscular. His face had those chiseled features. He had double thick eyelashes that lay gently around his dark brown eyes. Out of nowhere Connie questioned, *why do guys always have super long eyelashes, and we girls struggle to get those lashes out of a tube of mascara?* He was handsome all right! His teeth were strong and even, and when he smiled, you were doubly drawn to his dimples. *Why did he have to have dimples?*

Otis knew how slow Mondays were, so he came prepared. He tucked his drawing tablet under his arm this morning, and bought it along to the shop. *At least*, he thought, *I can work on sketches for Connie's bathroom.* He had come up with the idea to use the left inside wall of her closet to cut an opening for the door.

He knew she had cleared out the right side of the closet, but that was an outside wall. He was pretty sure the plumbing that extended from the kitchen to the bathroom was routed on the outside wall too. He thought the better way to go was to cut into the pantry wall about three feet to make a nice little walk through. All he needed was some two by fours, and sheet rock to put up the additional wall. The revisions would cause Connie to lose about two feet of closet space, and he would have to install another pole on the back wall for her clothes.

Otis turned to a fresh sheet in the sketchpad, and reached for his pencil and ruler. He had just begun to sketch his idea when the hanging bell at the top of the door post sounded. He looked up to see Connie, and his pulse quickened. He stood up from the worktable and stepped over to the counter. They both stared at each other for a second or two, and then Connie said, "Hi. Surprise!"

Otis was stumbling for his words.

"Hey. I didn't expect to see you here. I mean I didn't expect to see you at all, I mean… that is at all, today." Connie smiled, and looked around the small shop. It had built in shelving to store the TVs and other items he worked on. There was a long narrow room behind the bench where he worked. It didn't have a door, but there were strands of wooden beads hanging in front of a sheer curtain over the entryway. It appeared to be where he kept immediate supplies. The other door to the right, she surmised was the restroom. There was a small hallway that led to another closed door which could have been a supply closet.

"Well, I was in the area and wanted to drop in. This is nice." "Thank you, I'm sure you're just being kind. I would have cleaned up if I knew you were coming by." "Why? It looks okay to me." "Thanks again. I would give you the fifty-cent tour, but you can basically see the whole place from where you're standing. Here, come have a seat." Otis came from behind the counter, and walked Connie over to one of the two chairs sitting in front of the window that had the air-conditioner unit in it.

She noticed the little niche on the left hand wall near the front of the shop. It was nicely arranged and had a sign over it that read: **For Sale**. Her eyes fell on something she needed to purchase, but pushed that to the back of her mind until she had finished doing what she came to do. Before she could work up the nerve to what she wanted to say, Otis said he was glad she stopped by because there was something he'd like to share with her.

It was amazing how much their thoughts were in sync with each other. But, they knew it wasn't them as much as it was the Holy Spirit within them. They both agreed that they didn't mind some affection between the two of them, but *necking* and *heavy petting* was out.

Connie suddenly remembered the parking meter, and thought she should put some more money in it just to be on the safe side. Otis had an idea that was even better. He asked Connie if she felt like having lunch. He jokingly said, "I went to bed last night filled up on love, but I'm hungry today!" He took down the sign that hung in the window. That sign read: <u>We Are Open – Come</u> <u>on</u> <u>In</u>. The reverse side of card read: <u>Sorry – *We Are Close*</u>. He went behind the counter and picked up the other sign that read: <u>Be Back in One</u> <u>Hour</u>. He locked up, and walked Connie across to Street to 'Imperial Gardens' and then he jogged up the street and put more money in the parking meter.

It didn't take long for their order to arrive. They sat in the small Dine-In area near the front. Otis sat across from Connie in the chair facing the window. He said that way, he could see if anyone was stopping at the shop. He also said, since he was having lunch with her, they were going to do what the sign said–take the whole hour. He asked if Connie wanted to go back over to the shop after lunch. He had made a couple of sketches and he wanted to see what she thought of them. She said yes for two reasons. One, because she was excited to see the ideas he came up with, and the other was because she saw something on the little shelf she wanted to purchase.

When they got back to his shop Connie congratulated him on the section he'd put in for little gadgets that people might want to purchase. Most of the items were related to his business, and it kept customers from having to go to the big department store to purchase them. He had record player needles, colorful spindles, wall hooks, extension cords, new transistor radios, and a section of 45s.

Behind the counter he sold the TV Guide, and on the countertop was a variety of candy bars. Connie asked him why he didn't sell chewing gum. He laughed and, told her that chewing gum was one of his weaknesses, and he was trying to quit chewing it because gum was pulling out his dental work. They stood at the door talking for a few minutes more, and Connie invited him for dinner on Tuesday.

Otis thought about the photo of her still laying on his work table. His first thought was to give it to her, but he didn't. Connie said she would cook him chicken again if he promised to bring along a dessert. Otis lifted his right arm high in the air, twisted his wrists towards him as if holding a tray or platter propped on the tips of his fingers, and said, "I'm on your doorstep already." Remembering they were standing in front of the door window, he gave her hand a light squeeze, and kissed her on the cheek.

Chapter 31

Tuesday's weren't busy days either, and Otis couldn't wait until the clock struck five o'clock. He was tempted to leave early, but was glad he didn't because out of the blue a business deal walked in the door and fell into his lap. He had been praying about more income if he was going to get married. He needed to the able to support a wife. His long-term plan was to expand his business, but he needed something to expand it with.

Evidentially his reputation for doing excellent repairs and service reached the ears of a certain well-known appliance store in town. Their customers brought brand new items from them, but when something went wrong with the merchandise, the stores didn't have anyone local to do repairs. They would have to send it back to the manufacture with the warranty, and sometimes it would take weeks, even months to get the item back. Some of their customers didn't mind, but most of them didn't want to wait that long. More than once, the store manager heard from their customers they didn't want to wait that long, so they were going to take their radio or TV to OD's Supply and Repair. They bragged on the excellent work, and customer service.

The store manager wanted to set up a contract with Otis to be there in-house repair person. He wouldn't have to go to them. They would deliver the merchandise to his shop, and would also pay him to repair anything that went wrong with their display models on the floor. That included things like toasters, blenders, and mixers; etc. It was extra money for sure, but he had to ask himself how would that help to expand his own business? Of course the money would help, but that wasn't the niche he thought he needed.

At dinner that evening he filled Connie in on the proposal, and asked if she had any ideas. He figured since she had a degree in business two heads were better than one. They were still discussing the matter while clearing the dishes from the dinner table. That's when Connie came up with a brilliant suggestion. "Why not throw in the deal that when they have their turn-over of new floor models, you get first *'dib's'* on last year's models. You could either bid on them, or agree to pay their last year's wholesale price. They wouldn't make the profit they would get from selling them retail, but then again, they would need the immediate floor space for the newer models coming in." She said it was bound to be cheaper than I could get it for my wholesale price, because I would be buying in bulk.

Otis stopped what he was doing, and swooped Connie off her feet. He swung her around in the air. "You're a genius, he said. I can tell we are going to be good together."

Otis showed Connie the sketches for the renovations. She was surprised how professional they looked. They were so precise they could have passed for blueprints. Connie wanted to talk about his fee, but he wouldn't hear of it. They agreed that if she paid for the

materials, his labor was free. "After all, he said, how would it look if I charged my fiancée for doing repairs?" He thought he said that in his mind, but from the expression on Connie's face, he realized he had voiced it out loud. "Oh, I'm sorry. I was thinking it
in my mind, and I didn't intend to say that out loud."

"Well, Connie said, you know what the *Word* says… "*What comes out of the mouth proceeds from the heart.*"
"Then… You're not upset about what I was thinking."
"No. As a matter of fact, it sounded pretty good to me."
Otis was anxious to seal it with a kiss, and that's exactly what he did. It wasn't a brush on the lips, and it wasn't a quick one either.
This time he lingered!

Otis and Connie knew their relationship had jumped to a whole new level, and if it seemed to be moving at a much faster pace than they expected. They sat in Connie's living room and talked about what this new phase really meant. Otis made it clear that he wasn't a *dater.*
In other words, he didn't date a woman just to say he went out on a date. He was looking for a wife–not a roommate. Connie agreed she felt the same way. She wasn't out there trying to date every Tom, Dick, and Harry just to see if they were the *right fit*. If she dated anyone, it was because she felt led of the Lord, and most likely he was her husband to be. She said 'Yes' because she loved him. Otis knew he not only loved Connie, but was *in* love with her, and he asked her to be his wife.

Otis apologized that he wasn't prepared with a ring, and didn't bend down on one knee. This was totally unplanned, and happened so suddenly. *However, he knew in the back of his mind, he was more prepared than Constance Webster thought he was.*

They agreed the next move was to set up a conference with Pastor and Sister Thornton. When Otis got home, although it was late he made a phone call to Olivia.

Olivia was ecstatic! When she got up Wednesday morning, she was able to put her hands on the item that Otis wanted. On his way into work, he drove by her house and picked the package up. He had so much running through his mind. It was overwhelming! As soon as he opened up for business, he called Pastor Thornton to see if he could allow him a few minutes of his time before Bible study. Otis wanted to ask his advice on the business offer, and to share his great news about him and Connie.

The next thing he did was to call the manager of the Appliance Store, and Otis told him the additional agreement he wanted to be in the contract. The man said it didn't seem like a problem to him. Otis said if all went well, he would have an answer for the store manager by the end of the week.

Pastor Thornton said he could have one of the church's attorneys to look over the contract for him, and Otis said he would have it on his desk the first thing tomorrow morning. As for the other thing Otis wanted to do, Pastor Thornton called his wife into the office so he could run the idea by her. She would know more about how women felt when it came to those things. Mrs. Thornton said she could only speak in general about his idea, and every woman was different. She admitted that she only knew Connie for a short two and a half months, but since they had already pledged their betrothal to each other, and she already said 'yes', it probably would be okay.

However, Mrs. Thornton did say his plan might work better tonight at mid-week Bible study, rather than in a large Sunday morning setting.

Pastor Thornton thought this situation was ironic, because he was going to be teaching about Jacob and Rachel this evening. It couldn't have been better planned! This was one of the greatest love stories in the Bible, and yet it would be unfolding in front of their very eyes tonight. It fit even down to Otis being tricked by his first wife, and the fourteen year wait between the time he could have been married to Constance, and their engagement on this week.

During Bible study Connie sat next to Olivia and Earl, and Otis sat on the same row, but on the other side of Edmund. When the study was over Pastor Thornton stepped down from the roster onto the main floor. He asked how everyone enjoyed the teaching for this evening. A lot of applause and Amens filled the sanctuary. Then he asked Constance to come up to the front.

"I'm sure those of you who have their family roots in this church know, or have known of the Webster family." At that moment he gave recognition to Pastor and Sister Dixon on the front pew. They were the under Shepherds of the congregation when Connie was just a little girl. Connie stood there politely with a smile fixed on her face. Pastor Thornton asked everyone to stay seated for a minute, and he would give the benediction after a special announcement. Connie had a puzzled look on her face because she knew she didn't have a special announcement.

So, she didn't know what special announcement he was talking about. Otis stood up and started walking up the middle aisle of the church. Connie got very nervous, and her stomach began to flutter. He suddenly stopped, did an about face, founding the pew where Mrs. Miller was sitting. He whispered something in her ear, and she lit up like a Christmas tree. Mrs. Miller waved her hands in the air saying, "Thank you Jesus!"

Otis came out from the pew and said, "I just wanted to keep my word to someone."

He came to the front of the church and standing directly in front of her, pulled a small box out of his pocket, and got down on one knee. *Oh no*, she said to herself. *He's going to propose to me in front of everybody.* He opened the lid of the box to expose a beautiful diamond ring. He said, "I Love You Constance Webster. Will You Marry Me?" She was floored. What could she say? She had already said *yes*, so she said "Yes" again.

All of a sudden there was the flash of a camera going off. *What in the world?* Who would have come to Bible study with a camera? When her eyes focused again, Levee was holding Earl's camera. She smiled a big smile at her sister giving her a big thumbs-up. Otis put the ring on Connie's finger, and it was a perfect fit.

Chapter 32

Otis and I called each other twice a day. You would think we would have run out of things to talk about, but we didn't. On one of those phone calls, I asked Otis how he was able to purchase a ring for me so quickly. Then he told me the story behind my engagement ring.

It turned out he had actually purchase the ring for me fourteen years ago when I was off at college. That was the summer our relationship got interrupted with, shall I say *worldly* things. We broke off going *steady,* and after I went back to school I never called him again. I met Anthony during that year. We dated for the next year and a half until we graduated, and then we got married.

Otis said he gave the engagement ring to my mother for safe keeping. After Belinda hounded him about wanting to become engaged, he finally gave in. He said he bought another ring for her, because he refused to let another woman where what was intended for me. After he and his wife divorced, he said he used to drop by the house often just to be around loving and caring folks.

I was flabbergasted. I must have seen the ring before, but didn't remember actually seeing it. It was when we siblings were going through mother's things after her death. She had pieces of jewelry that she wore often, and some pieces she never wore it all. Knowing this to be true, it never fazed me when Levee asked if she could keep that particular ring.

I couldn't believe that this engagement ring had waited for me for fourteen years. Not only that, but Otis said after he had made such a horrible mistake the first time, he began to pray to God and ask only for the '*good thing*' the Bible talks about coming into his life.

It wasn't a very popular thing that occurred back in the early 1970s, but we made an appointment with our pastor to receive some marital counseling. He said he was happy to see we were mature enough to have discussed through a lot of issues on our own. Pastor Thornton said it made it easier on him, because we already agreed on most of the things he would have presented to us in the sessions.

Even so, because we both had previous marriages, and now had been single and independent for so many years, he advised us not to rush the wedding date. "*Love* can happen quickly, he said, but old habits are hard to break."

Now that we had crossed that bridge, we felt the need to reconsider how much time we would spend together, alone. Levee and Earl invited us over for dinner and a game of Scrabble the last Sunday in September. It was a fun evening, and as they say, "*all's fair in love and war.*" Edmund and I ended up owning most of the properties, and we *racked* in big money. Otis was a good loser. He played it off by saying; "When we get married, you're handling the family finances!"

Time was moving on. It was late September, and October was just around the corner. We didn't have to keep a regular schedule of counseling with the Pastor; at least not yet. He said he wanted us to enjoy the freedom of our first few months of being engaged; however he and Mrs. Thornton would give us a call every so often just to see how things were going. They were there if we needed them.

Otis and I discussed a lot of things. We set the month of June for the wedding. We put our heads together to make a decision about our properties. He suggested we could both put both of the houses up for sale, and purchase a different house for the both of us, or he could sell his house and he would move into mine. Those were the best choices. Back then it wasn't a popular thing for a man to move into a house a woman owned, but Otis said he would never ask me to live in the house he and Belinda lived in. He still had some problems with calling her his *wife*. He said it in a jokingly way, but I know he was serious when he said,
"I just don't want any of her lingering evil spirits to come back to haunt our marriage."

Anyway, my parent's house was paid for. We only had the property taxes and utilities as expenses. No use starting out with new debt that wasn't necessary. I thought I would wait until after the holidays to make any changes to the downstairs bathroom. I had some finances put away, but I wanted to use them for Thanksgiving and Christmas. I applied for a part-time job. It was way past my time to start new cash flow coming into the house, but before I started, I wanted to visit my friend Sylvia in Memphis. We had only talked a few times since I'd been

259

back home, and maybe this visit would do me some good before the winter months set in.

Otis did a little remodeling to the front of the shop. He took down the wall shelves he had built, and moved the items he had repaired for his customers to the narrow room with the beaded curtains. That left room for the new racks he ordered to put his small appliances on, and it also left ample space for the larger floor items. The 'L' shaped corner wall was 11' x 5'.

I dropped by the store to see how things were coming along. It had been two weeks since Otis had accepted the contract from the Appliance Store, and things were looking great. The new shelving racks and a couple of TVs lined up against the wall gave his business a feel of expansion. Otis said the two television sets on the floor, and the one radio on the top shelf of the rack belonged to the other store. He showed me the sketches he finished drawing for a new windows sign to advertise the shop would be carrying new TVs, radios, and small appliances. He was going to take it to the printers that evening after he closed. I told him how much I was going to miss sitting beside him in Bible study tomorrow night, and he said he hoped he could go two and
a half days without seeing me, or hearing my voice.

I told Otis I was leaving for Sylvia's the first thing in the morning and should be in Memphis around One o'clock in the afternoon. If all went well I should be back home Friday afternoon. We said how much we would miss each other. We embraced in an endearing kiss, and said our "goodbyes".

By that evening Connie wanted to hear Otis's voice. He couldn't call her, because she didn't give him Sylvia's telephone number. Connie had his number at the shop and his home number, but she had to see if she had the strength to wait until she got back home to call him. By Thursday morning Sylvia had heard Otis's name so many times, she told Connie to telephone him so she could get some peace. Connie got the message.

She tried to enjoy herself, but she had Otis on the brain so much so, that Sylvia said if she wrapped some photo paper around Connie's head, it would probably print out a picture of Otis. The college buddies went to a museum there in Memphis, out to dinner, and then to a movie. By Thursday evening, they were so exhausted they decided to stay around the house. They lounged in their pajamas looking through their old college yearbook. The subject of Otis slipped from Connie's lips again, and Sylvia said she couldn't believe this was the *same* Otis Connie said she would never talk to again fourteen years ago. They both laughed at how their life plans had changed over the years, and almost at the same time they said: "*Never say, never*!"

Otis muddled through Wednesday night Bible study. He picked up his new sign for the window on Thursday morning. He centered the sign in the large window affixing it with those clear, plastic suction cups. Almost immediately people began to respond the sign. He knew he had to stay focused on the business of the day, which would be the only thing to keep his mind off of Connie. His scheduled repairs were ready for pickup, so he concentrated on shifting things around to make the shop seem more appealing. That wasn't much help either because it made him think of Connie again. She had such a flare for design and decorating. The store radio was playing softly in the background, and the song that came on pricked his heart even the more. It was "Shadows without Pity", sung by Perry Como. Como's voice slowly crooned out the words:

> *"... Yesterday I shut my eyes, face up to the clouds, drinking in the rain, but your image still was there, floating in the air brighter than a flame. Yesterday I saw a city, full of shadows without pity–and I heard a steady rain whispering your name... whispering Your Name."*

"That does it! Otis said. I'm going to find a way to call Connie." He went behind the counter to use the store telephone.

If I call the operator, maybe I can get her girlfriend's telephone number. I know her name is Sylvia Carter, and she lives in Memphis. After all, how many Sylvia Carter's can there be living in Memphis?

He reached for the telephone, and the jingle of the bell above the door sounded. He looked up to see a guy wearing an emblem on his shirt just like the one the

Appliance Center uses for their workers. He said, "Excuse me sir, I'm looking for a…for a, he looked down at his clipboard, a Otis Delaney." Otis' gazed behind the young man to a huge truck in front of the store. There was an orange traffic cone in the back of it, but it still was blocking traffic. Otis looked at the order on the clipboard and thought there must be some sort of mistake. The price was what he had negotiated on, but this guy had far more TVs and appliances than he had expected.

To be honest, he didn't know what he was bidding on that day when he placed his bid for the floor model merchandise. Evidentially, it also included the unboxed merchandise in the storeroom that was the same as the floor model sampled. This was unbelievable! No wonder the manager kept saying to him, "You drive a hard bargain."

Otis spent more money than he had expected to spend, but he thought he would just have to make less profit on the merchandise he negotiated for.

He called Edmund to help him unload the small appliances and the floor model TVs. He had (1) black and white, (2) color TV's in their console cabinets, and (1) color freestanding floor model TV. There was a display model of a portable color TV, a few alarm clock radios, a blender with bowl set, and mixers, and (2) electric shaver's with Rollo blades packaged in their carrying case. Otis had to close the shop while the delivery guy got permission from his boss to follow him home with the truck. He had to use his garage to store the unboxed merchandise.

Otis spent the rest of the day rearranging things at the shop. That afternoon he thought of Connie for a different reason. Someone had to help him update his ledgers, code the merchandise, breakdown the individual cost, and price it for retail sales. Otis didn't leave the shop until after 7 p.m.

He was tired, and his back was hurting. He knew that one of the first things he would purchase four this increasing volume of business would be a *furniture dolly*. He also knew that Friday evening may be a more than usual busy day. He already had curiosity coming from the business owners on the street. When his customers came in to pick up their repairs, they looked at some of the new merchandise and wondered if they could make purchases right away. He explained he just got the items in, and they had to be catalogued and ticketed as inventory first. But the new merchandise would be ready for sale on Friday.

Chapter 33

Otis woke up in a slight panic. He still couldn't open the shop at nine o'clock today and have the new merchandise ready for sale. Maybe he could go down to the shop, and put a sign on the door that the shop would be close until tomorrow. But he thought that was no way to start the first day of blessings the Lord allowed to come his way to expand his business. He knew it was early, but he called the operator to get a long distance number. Good! There were only two people listed in the Memphis directory under that name.

Sylvia was startled by the ring of the telephone. Her bleary eyes tried to focus on the digital numbers of the clock radio, 7:15 a.m. "Who could be calling me at this hour of the morning?" Her first thought went to Connie. *Was there something wrong? What had happened?* She answered the phone to hear a man's voice. It was Otis Delaney. He apologized for calling at such an early hour, but he wanted to know if he caught Connie before she left.

She said that he and Connie must really be in love with each other, because she left last night about 11 o'clock. Sylvia said they were lounging around talking, and all of a sudden she got dressed and said she had to leave, that she couldn't even spend the night. Sylvia said Connie told her she would just have to get some sleep when she got home. From as much as she could judge time-wise, Connie should have gotten back home around 6:00 a.m. that morning.

When the telephone rang, Connie thought she had been asleep for four or five hours. She was so excited to hear Otis's voice she didn't realize she had only slept for about two and a half hours. "Wait a minute, how did you know I was home?" Otis confessed he'd called Sylvia early that morning. He said he felt badly now, because he forgot that the Memphis time zone was one hour behind Georgia's. He explained what happened on yesterday, rushing through some things, and leaving out others. He really needed her help to set up his books in a more professional way. The clock showed 8:20 a.m. She told Otis not to panic, to open the shop on time. She would meet him there at nine o'clock. He said she could park in the rear of the store where each shop had its reserved parking spots.

Connie knew the sleep she missed out on would catch up with her later during the day, but right now her thoughts were reeling. How to pull the shop together quickly enough for Otis to be able to start sales on his new merchandise when he opened?

Connie knocked on the back door of the shop. Otis opened the door and literally fell into her arms. "Thank you, thank you, thank you, he said. I love you *sooo* much." Connie was bemused, but it was pleasing to know that someone missed you, and needed you. Otis gave her all the papers, and invoices he received up to that point. She got right to work. What was overwhelming to him, seemed to flow like clockwork with her. He knew the workers came in at the Imperial Gardens around nine-thirty in the morning, so he jolted across to street to get them two cups of coffee.

A few store owners on the block poked their heads in the door to congratulate him on the new venture he was undertaking, but for the most part, the morning remained calm. His general business on Friday didn't picked up until after 4 p.m. when customers came in to get their repaired merchandise, or to browse around after work. Connie worked effortlessly at the ledgers, recording items into different books. Otis's job was to make sure the item number recorded in the sales ledger matched the item number on the ticket, and that the particular tickets got onto the right merchandise. They checked, and double checked again.

By 12 o'clock noon they both needed to eat something, but neither one of them wanted to stop working. Otis asked if it going to be pizza, or Chinese. They chose pizza. He called in the order, and Connie teased him saying, "You know, the next time I help you out, I expect to be paid more than a slice of pizza."

Otis came over to where she was sitting behind his desk and gave her a big kiss on the forehand, one on the cheek, and then gallantly he kissed the back of her hand. She said, "Thank you *kind sir*, I've been well paid." At that moment, Otis got a brilliant idea.

"Hey, didn't you say you were looking for a part-time job? Well, how about working for me? It's evident the store is going to become quite busy, and I won't be able to do repairs for the Appliance Center, repairs for my regular clientele, and wait on new customers. It will only be a few days a week, and besides I can vouch for the handsome, debonair store manager. We'll get to be together more."

"It sounds good, but it's the being together more that I'm worried about." "Hey, wha-cha trying to say, you don't want to be with me?"
"No, but that's just the problem she said bashfully. I do want to be with you. "Well, well, well", he said raising his eyebrows up and down, and making pretend he was stroking a non-existing goatee. Connie laughed. Then he said, "Can you at least pray about it. I missed you so much over the last couple of days I don't know how I'm going to make it through 'till June."

"I've already prayed about some of that. That's why I came back early. I missed you so much too, and if it's all right with you, we can talk to Pastor Thornton about moving our wedding date to this coming February. We would have been seeing each other for more than five months, and we can ask him if February 12th is clear on his calendar."
"Baby, you don't know how great that sounds to me." Otis leaned in to give her a kiss just as the ding-a-ling of the bell sounded. His kiss was halted, and he looked up to see the delivery guy from down the street standing in the doorway with a large flat box in his hand. "Somebody here order a pizza?"

———

Every time Connie took a bite of her pizza, the scenario of the irritated look on Otis's face played over and over again. It wasn't just the look, but it was what he said about the bell after the delivery boy left out; something about ripping that *stupid* bell off its hook. Connie wrote a reminder on the post-it notepad. *Otis wants me to fill out a 1099 form for tax purposes.* After lunch Otis and Connie took time to read labels, the information printed on the backs of boxes, the directions and warrantees having to do with the new appliances. They were glad they used that time wisely, because Otis was right. By four o'clock word had gotten around concerning the new merchandise in his shop.

Connie was prepared to write up customer receipts. While Otis showed features on certain items, and compared his low prices to that of his discount store competitors. Most small appliance items were ready and waiting on shelves, or in the storage room. They set up a lay-a-way plan for large ticket items the customers were not able to purchase in full.

On Sunday Otis spoke with Pastor Thornton about all the changes that had occurred. He didn't see any problem with their changing the date of the wedding. As a matter of fact, he told them it probably was in God's plan anyway. Now they would have an opportunity to work with each other several times a week, and not only that, but they could determine how well they worked together as a couple under extreme pressure. He said it wouldn't surprise him one bit if they figured out that what they thought was their plan, was God's plan all along. If He was able to preserve their love for each other these fourteen years–surely He could keep them for the next three months.

That proved to be true. Business was booming during the holidays. We were looking for a larger building for OD's Appliance and Repairs. It would probably be one of those storefronts in the strip mall. Otis had a 'For Sale' sign up in front of his house. If it sold before our wedding date, he would rent another apartment until that time came.

We had Thanksgiving at Levee's, and Christmas was at my house. Levee had the baby two days after Thanksgiving, so she was able to visit by then. Otis put in a bid for the after winter clearance sale items at the Appliance Center. If all went well, that shipment would be delivered in March. Levee and I were planning the wedding, and Otis was planning the honeymoon. I have never gone on a cruise before, but he told me cruises were very romantic. I didn't know where we were going however, Otis said we would probably have to book another cruise if I wanted to visit any of the ports. He said we probably wouldn't get off the ship much this first time around.

At the first of the year Levee began to walk me through some of the things I would need to do in order to change my name on personal documents. It felt a little odd having your little sister walk you through some things. Some things I remembered from the first time I got married, but it was nice to have my sister help me out. Otis would have been in the larger store by the time our honeymoon came around, but he wanted to keep the store open. The plan was for Edmund and his lady friend Rachel to run to run things while we honeymooned. Edmund was used to running things at the Flee Market, so Otis walked him through a few things concerning OD's Appliance and Repairs.

When does love flourish? Who knows! It's just like one of the Supremes song of 1966 said, ('*You Can't Hurry Love*' you just have to wait.) I've learned that going ahead of God just doesn't work. But I also learned this…you may have to wait, one, two, or even ten years. But one thing is for sure, when it comes to '*Matters of the Heart*', God always has your back.

Lucy introduced her readers to the Amish community in 2012 with her first novel *Rachel's Forbidden Love.* The sequel to *Rachel's Forbidden Love; The Reunion* in 2014, and a new platform in her romance novels with *Pastor Q and Donna*, 2014, *The Last Time I saw Love*, 2015, *Matters of the Heart,* 2017, and *The Best Christmas Ever* in 2019. Three novels have sinced been revised in 2020, and 2021 under her newly formed company, A Novel Thing LLC.

Lucy used her love for writing, and her dedication to Christian values to reintroduce the Christian Romance Novel to a new generation of readers. Her belief is that chivalry is not dead, and every lady still looks forward to the passionate *woo* of romance. Heath's writing talents take the reader on a journey of romantic nuances that causes them to cheer for the hero, and heroine as they endeavor to find the true love God has planned for them.

Heath now resides in Lithonia, Ga., and comes from a family of ten siblings. She always appreciated her parents instilling in their children a sense of integrity, and commitment. It wasn't a matter of *where* you lived, but *how* you lived.

lorene@mail2world.com
http://anovelthing.webnode.com
Barnesandnoble.com, Amazonbooks.com, kindle ebook.com